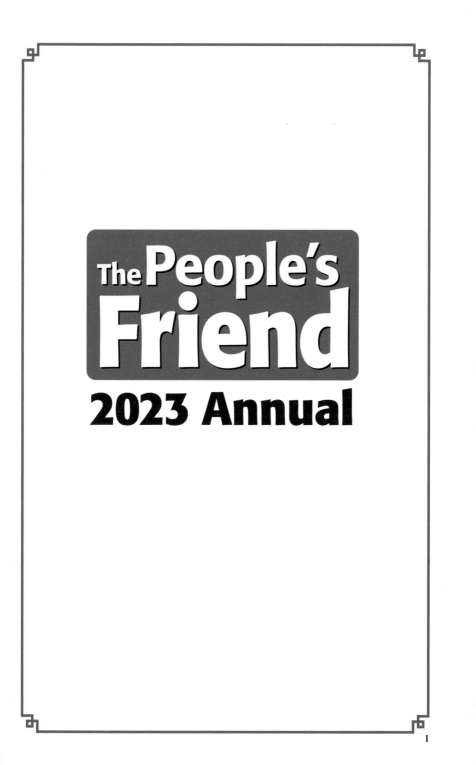

The People's Friend

2023 Annual

Waterford, Ireland

Founded in 914 AD, Ireland's oldest city, Waterford, celebrates its past while looking to the future with a vibrant cultural feel.

It's hardly surprising the strategic setting of this south-eastern seaport city made the Vikings want to lay down roots, building not only a dock, but also a tower in what is now known as the Viking Triangle. The Anglo-Normans are thought to have built upon that earlier structure, and Reginald's Tower is Ireland's oldest civic building.

Parts of the old walled city remain, serving as a reminder of a turbulent past in which the inhabitants tried to safeguard against attack. Within those walls, industry changed and adapted over the centuries, but what really put Waterford on the world map was, of course, its famed crystal, which George and William Penrose began making in 1783.

Today there's much to see and do, from beautiful architecture to exceptional restaurants. One great way to soak up the atmosphere while delving into the fascinating past is with a guided walking tour.

Contents

Dear Readers . . .

Welcome to "The People's Friend" Annual 2023, which is packed with a wealth of wonderful reading to touch your heart.

We have 25 brand-new stories by favourite authors, all accompanied by stunning colour illustrations, and a selection of uplifting and inspiring poems.

Inside you'll also find some of J. Campbell Kerr's finest watercolour paintings and a treasure trove of fascinating vintage household hints and tips collected from the magazine's archives.

I hope you enjoy reading it!

Angela

Angela Gilchrist, Editor

Poetry

J. Campbell Kerr Paintings

Vintage Cleaning Tips

A Year To Remember

by Kate Blackadder

I T was the winter of 1947 all over again – only, thank goodness, there wasn't the worry of keeping a new baby warm and getting nappies dry.

At any time of year Maggie shivered when she remembered that awful time in her life. But the living-room was icy cold this morning, too, and it looked as if the wind must have been coming down the chimney.

Maggie blinked and coughed in the smoke that blew into her face when she tried to coax life into the fire.

Eventually she gave up the fight and got to her feet awkwardly, it being rather difficult to move in her many layers of clothes, which included a pair of Iain's long johns under her tweed skirt, and on top a woolly vest and two woolly jumpers – very appropriate for a sheep farmer's wife!

How she was going to get her coat on top of all that when she went outside was a problem she'd face shortly, but Maggie knew it was a minor problem in the grand scale of things.

Running footsteps overhead indicated that Carmel was awake and had dashed to the freezing bathroom and back to get dressed in her bedroom.

No point in worrying her yet about her dad.

When Carmel's steps sounded on the stairs Maggie went to the kitchen and ladled out a bowl of porridge. She had a little brown sugar left over from making the black bun, so as a birthday treat she sprinkled some on top.

"Mmm, thanks, Mum." Carmel lifted Tabby off the chair beside the Rayburn and sat huddled into its warmth, cat on her knee and porridge bowl in hand.

"Happy birthday, dear." Maggie dropped a kiss on Carmel's head. "It's as snowy as it was the day you were born. Your dad didn't have a car then, but he walked over the hill and borrowed Jock MacFarlane's Morris so he could fetch the midwife.

"Those four hours before he came back with her were the longest of

Illustration by Gerard Fay.

my entire life.

"She ended up staying with us until the third of January, when the snowplough got to the farm road. There'll never be a New Year like that one!"

Carmel heard this story every year, with excitement when she was younger, but now she listened, Maggie could see, with affectionate indulgence.

"And when I eventually arrived you asked the midwife what her name was, because you wanted to call me after her to say thank you, and even when she told you, you still –"

"Her mother was Irish. I thought it was a lovely name," Maggie interrupted.

Carmel screwed up her face.

"The boys at school call me Caramel. Or, even worse, Camel." She tipped Tabby on to the floor, took her bowl over to the sink and looked out of the window.

"What's Dad doing?"

Maggie put Tabby back on the chair.

"Do you want to open your parcels now?"

The presents included a pair of boots Carmel had begged for after seeing them in a catalogue – ridiculous things in Maggie's opinion, more like shoes with stretchy leather socks attached. Totally impractical for a country girl.

"I'll wait for Dad," Carmel replied. "Is he out in that weather?"

Daddy's girl. Ever since she could hold on to Iain's finger, Carmel had wanted to follow him around the farm and would cry when he had to go without her.

Maggie turned round.

"One of Jock's grandsons appeared just after light. You didn't hear him knocking?"

"Which grandson?" Carmel asked casually as she smoothed her hair back.

"Fergus, I think. There was something wrong with a cow and they couldn't ring the vet as the telephone lines are down, so he came for your dad," Maggie explained. "He drove the tractor as far as he could, then carved himself a path with a shovel."

Carmel peered out.

"I can't see a path. It must have got filled in again."

Maggie was trying not to think about that, or about the two miles between here and the MacFarlane place.

"Let's get on with the outdoor chores," she said briskly. "We'll feed the sheep together, then I'll do the dogs if you'll see to the hens.

"Oh, and if you see Treacle, bring her in. This is no weather for a cat to be outside."

Carmel wore stretch slacks with a pair of her father's thick kilt socks over them. Her top half looked as padded as Maggie's own.

They couldn't help laughing as they struggled into wellies and coats in the back lobby, falling against each other like a couple of skittles.

After they'd added scarves, hats and gloves, Maggie took a deep breath and opened the door.

What was that poem, about the wind being like a whetted knife? The weatherman on the wireless this morning had got it right.

It was even colder than that winter 15 years ago, biting into any piece of exposed skin.

Two hours later they staggered in, shutting the door behind them with a joint effort.

"Your dad's not back yet." Maggie looked at the hook where his jacket would be. "I'll get the broth started and you could do those sausage rolls you made in your Homecraft class. And some shortbread?

"There surely won't be any first-footers tonight in this weather, but we'll have a Hogmanay birthday party, just the three of us."

She put up a silent prayer that Iain would get back safely.

"I'll try lighting that fire again."

This time, with the boost of some buttery paper, it caught light. She put on the fireguard, and as she stood up she caught sight of the card on the mantelpiece sent by midwife Carmel, now in faraway British Columbia.

Greetings across the miles, it said on the front, and inside she'd written, *How's my baby girl? There's never been a New Year like that one, has there?*

She was right, Maggie thought, remembering the long hours before the baby's arrival at five to midnight, and her gratitude for the young midwife's skill and cheery disposition.

✳   ✳   ✳   ✳

At three o'clock they sat down for a cup of tea and, in Carmel's case, several sausage rolls.

Maggie couldn't eat a thing.

"I'll have one later," she said, looking for the umpteenth time out of the window, willing Iain to appear out of the gloom.

"What's that noise?" Carmel asked suddenly, tipping her head to one side. "It can't be, but it sounds like someone's knocking on the front door."

Maggie listened, too.

"Maybe something's blowing against it."

None of their friends or neighbours ever came to the front – and none of them knocked, come to that. They pushed open the back door and called a greeting.

Maggie had to tug quite hard before the door rasped open.

On the step was a man whose features she vaguely recognised, although she couldn't have said from where.

On one side of him someone was pushing back the hood of a red quilted jacket, and on the other there were two much smaller figures.

"Maggie?" The owner of the red jacket beamed at her. "Surprise!"

"Surprise for us, too, I can assure you," the man added, and his transatlantic accent confirmed to Maggie that, as impossible as it seemed, the woman was midwife Carmel.

The snow drifting into the house galvanised her.

"Come in, come in." She held the door open for the couple, who ushered two children in front of them.

"I can't believe it. Carmel – Baby Carmel, this is the lovely lady who was the first person to hold you," Maggie declared.

"Baby" Carmel came forward shyly to say hello.

"These are my girls, Yvonne and Wendy, and my husband, Bob," Carmel said.

Maggie glanced at the mantelpiece. The photograph of her family that Carmel had included in her Christmas card was propped against the clock.

"We're so sorry to land on you like this," Bob said. "It wasn't what Carrie intended."

"Bob calls me Carrie – just as well to avoid the confusion of having two Carmels!" Carrie explained, taking off her jacket.

Maggie indicated to Carmel to put the kettle on.

"But how come you're here? I mean in Scotland, at this time of year?"

"Crazy, I know," Carrie replied. "Blame my sister – she had the

romantic notion to get married on Christmas Eve and wanted my girls to
be bridesmaids.

"We decided when we booked we'd stay over here for New Year, too,
– that was back in June when snow wasn't on our minds."

"The idea was to stay with a friend of Carrie's tonight and pop in to
surprise you on New Year's Day," Bob explained.

"But the snow's drifting and the signs are covered over – we weren't
sure we were on the right road.

"Then Carrie recognised that forked tree by your farm gate, so we
abandoned the car and walked up. I hope you can give us directions. I
have a map right here."

New Calendar

Squares all blank for me to fill:
Birthdays, weddings, what you will.
Dentist, doctor, holidays,
Theatre trips and special days.

January to July,
Look at how the weeks whizz by.
Grandson born a year ago;
Now he's crawling – watch him go!

August up to Bonfire Night,
Sparklers, fireworks set alight.
Wedding anniversary,
Then time to buy the Christmas tree.

Now I'm up to New Year's Eve –
What's this year got up its sleeve?
Squares all blank for me to fill –
Time that never does stand still.

Tessa-Jo Stone

Maggie looked at him and then at Carrie.

"Oh, my dears, I don't think you'll be going anywhere tonight. You must –"

"Mum!" Carmel's voice sounded squeaky.

"Excuse me," Maggie said to her unexpected guests and hurried into the kitchen.

Her husband and Fergus MacFarlane were standing there, dripping snow on to the floor, looking tired but very pleased with themselves.

Maggie hid her feelings under practicalities.

"There you are. For goodness' sake, take your jackets off. All well with the cow?"

"Yes, thanks, Mrs Wilson," Fergus replied.

"Fergus brought us back most of the way on the tractor, and we thought it would be safer for him to stay the night here than go back," Iain told his wife.

Out of the corner of her eye Maggie could see that Carmel, after laying a tray with cups and saucers, was stealthily removing the kilt socks and biting her lip.

The penny dropped. Well, Fergus was a good-looking lad.

"Of course," she said. "We'll have quite a party because –"

"Hold on, Mags," Iain interrupted. "Fergus will give me a hand with the chores, and then I believe we have a birthday to celebrate."

"Happy birthday, Caramel. I mean Carmel," Fergus said with a smile.

"Thanks." Carmel went bright red.

"Mum," she whispered urgently when Iain and Fergus went out. "I'll help them. Can I open that parcel and get my new boots?"

"To wear outside? Are you daft?" Maggie exclaimed. "They'd be ruined before you reached the fence.

"You're not going out unless you're properly clad, and that means thick socks and wellies, however unfashionable they are."

"Mu-um," Carmel wailed.

Maggie remembered how she had felt the first time she saw Iain, at a village dance at the end of the war.

"Go and put on something pretty," she told her. "Quickly now. We've beds to make up and guests to feed."

And, she thought as Carmel ran upstairs, she must change her own attire for something that made her look less like a scarecrow.

"Can I help you, Maggie?" Carrie had come into the kitchen. "I feel terrible landing on you like this."

"The more the merrier. I thought it would be only the three of us having a birthday tea and bringing in the New Year," Maggie replied. "Who better to celebrate with than you, for auld lang syne?"

*　*　*　*

The traditional New Year custom – of a dark-haired visitor bearing a lump of coal – was enacted in its own way before the witching hour when Iain and Fergus came in, the latter bearing a box in which were Treacle and three tiny black kittens, retrieved from a cold corner of the barn to sleep by the Rayburn.

When justice had been done to the spread she and Carmel had prepared, and the snow continued to hurl itself against the windows, Maggie put up a silent thank you.

She watched Iain and Bob put the world to rights, while Carmel and Fergus played Snap with the little girls, everyone safe and happy in front of the fire.

She turned to smile at Carrie, who was sitting beside her on the settee.

"So here we are again!" she exclaimed. "Another New Year just like that one!" ■

Polesden Lacey, Surrey

This grand Edwardian house, set in a 1,400-acre estate within the Surrey Hills, was once the playground of royalty such as King Edward VII. Situated just 25 miles from London, it proved the perfect escape, and society hostess and widow Margaret Greville regularly organised lavish parties for her regal guests. In fact, she was so fond of the Duke and Duchess of York that she allowed them exclusive use of her house for their honeymoon in 1923.

The ever-generous hostess bequeathed the house and grounds to the National Trust, ensuring visitors could enjoy the delights it has to offer. Take a stroll through the house and grounds, admiring the walled rose garden and other seasonal garden rooms, or enjoy a game of croquet.

Its beautiful setting has proved the perfect backdrop for filming productions such as Agatha Christie's "At Bertram's Hotel", and the gardens proved ideal for the "Jeeves And Wooster" series.

Always with an eye on maintaining the house and gardens for future generations, the Steinway piano in the Gold Room has been conserved, while work to restore the chalk grassland of the Polesden Valley aims to encourage more wildlife and insects, such as the Chalkhill blue butterfly.

Poor Aunt Izzie

by Susan Blackburn

O K, then, Hal. Thank you for letting me know. Leave it with me and I'll see what I can do." My usually unflappable dad looked bemused as he ended the call.

"Everything all right?" I asked.

"That was someone called Hal about your aunt Izzie, Tasha. I can't believe she has me down as her next of kin after all that happened. We lost touch years ago." Dad sat down heavily at the table.

"Evidently," he went on, "my sister has had a mild heart attack and ended up in hospital. The problem, Hal tells me, is there's nobody to care for her when she comes home."

"Nobody at all? Can't this Hal arrange something?"

"It would seem not – she can be stubborn. He was a bit desperate. That's why he contacted me." A worried frown creased his forehead.

"The thing is, love," my father mused later as we were having our evening meal, "Izzie is family, however long it is since I've seen her. For obvious reasons it can't be me who goes to look after her.

He looked at me hopefully.

"But you could."

I nearly choked on my chicken pie.

"Me?"

"I know, Tash, but just think about it. You're Izzie's niece, not to mention a qualified nurse. You've just split up with Jed, and you have been unsettled at the hospital lately . . ." Dad hesitated.

"A good temporary solution, maybe, while you think which direction you want to take?"

"But I don't know her, or anything about her," I protested.

"Nor do I, Tash," Dad said, sounding rather guilty. "I was about eleven when Izzie married someone my parents didn't approve of. She came home when it went pear-shaped, had a terrible row with them and stormed off.

"When my parents died a few years later – I was in my early twenties by then – I found her address amongst their papers. She'd settled somewhere in the wilds of the Yorkshire moors.

"I wrote to let her know and suggested it would be good to see her,

Illustration by Kirk Houston.

but she wrote back to say best not and I didn't push it. We'd never been close." Dad sighed. "But she is still at that same address. A lovely part of the country, I understand." He gave me a quizzical grin.

My break-up with Jed hadn't bothered me, but it had left a gap in my life, and Dad was right, I had been unsettled at work and had given in my notice.

Maybe looking after Aunt Izzie could be a good stopgap as I sorted myself out.

"But why has she no friends? It doesn't look good, Dad. She's probably quite mad," I said. "Another Miss Havisham?" I was an avid reader and loved Dickens.

Dad laughed.

"We could brave it together to make sure you won't be walking into the lion's den." He smiled. "Or Miss Havisham's wedding breakfast."

I giggled. How I adored my dad. It had been him and me against the world since my mum had died giving me life 28 years ago.

* * * *

"This Hal does seem to know her pretty well," Dad told me as he came off the phone a few days later. "And he said although she's proud and prickly, and, by preference, pretty much a loner, she's a lovely person. "But she's furious with Hal for suggesting she needs help. It'll take a bit of diplomacy to persuade her that you should go."

* * * *

The following week I pulled up at Aunt Izzie's place having decided, after a few conversations with her, plus Hal's testimonial, that I should be safe enough to go alone.

The cottage itself was gorgeous and had stunning views of the moors from every window. With its nooks, crannies and passageways, it was full of character.

Being a bookworm, I was delighted to find bookshelves crammed with novels of every genre, including murder mysteries, which I enjoyed above all.

I put the chicken casserole I'd brought with me in the oven to cook ready for Izzie's return, then set off the hospital in Raston, a largish town about 20 miles away.

"Hello," I said when I first laid eyes on the pale yet perfectly groomed figure of my aunt, sitting in a chair by her bed.

"Ah, Tasha, I presume," she replied.

"Now, Tom," she continued in a soft yet steely voice as she addressed the nurse clutching the handles of a wheelchair. "I am not, repeat not, getting into that contraption."

"Please, Izzie, if anything happened I'd be for it, now, wouldn't I?" came the harassed rejoinder.

"And you'll be for it if you try to get me in that thing," Izzie snapped. "I am quite capable of walking."

Tom sighed.

"Come on, then. Give me your arm. Let's get you out of here before you cause any more trouble."

He flashed a grin at Izzie.

The smile she gave him in return lit up her face, making me realise how attractive my aunt was. Despite what she'd been through, she looked a lot younger than her nearly seventy years.

Tom and I got Izzie settled in my car.

"Thank you, Tom," she said graciously. "You've been most kind."

And that was my introduction to Aunt Izzie.

Izzie dozed through the journey and I could tell, despite her bravado, that she was tired.

"Here we are," I said as I pulled into the driveway. "Home again."

* * * *

"I'm afraid I can't eat another morsel, delicious though this is," Izzie said as she put down her knife and fork, leaving much of her food unfinished.

I frowned.

"Are you OK, Aunt Izzie?" I asked casually, as I pottered around clearing the table.

Izzie glared at me.

"Shall we make a pact? Nurse or not, I want no fussing. I shall tell you if I feel unwell. Otherwise you can take it I'm fine. Understood?"

"Understood," I shot back. "But I shall be doing all the usual checks on you and administering your medication. Is that understood, Aunt Izzie?"

Izzie grinned.

"I think we shall do very well, Tasha," she said. "And please, it's Izzie."

I nodded.

"Well, Izzie, what about shopping? Where do you get your supplies?"

"There's a village about five miles further on from here with a good local shop. I usually go in for the paper and my daily shopping each morning. Perhaps you could take that over for the moment?"

"Of course," I said, relieved we weren't quite as isolated as I'd thought.

As Izzie had predicted, we did do very well, falling into a leisurely routine, starting with me taking Izzie her breakfast each morning.

"You needn't think you're going to supervise me whilst I shower and dress," Izzie huffed as she cracked open the top of her egg with unnecessary force the first morning. "I shall call you if I need you."

Once she was dressed she sat in the conservatory reading, whilst I nipped into the village. Then, after a light lunch, she didn't take much persuading to have a nap.

Afterwards she would hold my arm as we wandered around her beautiful walled garden.

Gradually we progressed to walks along the lane, breathing in the invigorating scent of the moors.

"What about you?" I asked curiously. "What do you do with yourself out here all alone?"

To my surprise, Izzie flushed and a guilty look crossed her face.

"This and that," she said abruptly. "Ah, here we are."

Well, that was weird, I thought, as she almost shot into the cottage.

The next morning we were enjoying our usual elevenses in the conservatory, Izzie absorbed in the paper and myself in a book, when we heard a vehicle approaching.

"Oh, no." Izzie groaned. "I told him I would let him know when to come."

"Is anyone home?" a cultured voice enquired.

A tall, broad-shouldered man came into view. My jaw dropped as he went over to Izzie and gave her a somewhat more than friendly kiss.

"Missed you so much, darling," I heard him murmur.

"What's going on, Izzie?"

"Well, my dear, this is Hal Crosskill." A slight pause. "Actually, he's my agent."

"Agent? But why would you need an agent?" I stuttered.

"Have you heard of R.I. Derekson, Tasha?"

"The thriller writer? I love her books and you've loads of them, haven't you?"

"Well, Tasha, dear, I am she. Ruth Isabella Derekson," Izzie announced, as if she was telling me it might rain later.

Suddenly everything slotted into place. I had rather wondered how Aunt Izzie had been funding her more than comfortable way of life.

"Hal has been my agent since my first novel." She blushed. "And lately he's become, well, a little more than a very good friend."

"I'm sorry if I've blown your cover, darling." Hal twinkled back at Izzie.

I suddenly felt as if I'd woken up in a parallel universe.

Hal turned to me.

"Izzie, being the proverbial loner, insists on remaining anonymous," he explained. "She made it clear to the publishers from the start that it would be me doing all the publicity for her novels."

He grinned.

"Being Izzie, she got her way."

"Right," I croaked.

I couldn't take this in. My aunt, a famous author – and romantically attached, too.

After I'd made coffee for us all, Hal stood up and stretched.

"Well, I must be on my way. I'll see you soon, Izzie." He bent and kissed her, then whispered something in her ear that made her blush and flap him away.

He laughed, then took my hand.

"Thank you for looking after Izzie so well," he said. "I wanted to myself, but she wouldn't hear of it."

"I should think not," Izzie put in. "You were far better employed seeing to my affairs, whilst my lovely niece looked after my every need."

At this she looked at me with such a loving smile I felt a warm glow.

"Now off you go, Hal, and I'll see you soon," Izzie said imperiously.

Hal laughed.

"I'm going. Bye, ladies." He strode to the door and with a final wave was gone.

I gazed at Izzie.

"Well," I said, "you have some explaining to do, Ms Derekson.

"How on earth," I asked her wonderingly, "did you become, well, who you are today?"

Izzie took a deep breath and began her story.

"I was always strong minded. Once it was made up I wouldn't be swayed. That didn't go down well with my parents, who were rigid, austere people, strict and unemotional.

"We never had a good relationship. Your father was a lot younger than me, much more placid, so he connected better with them on the whole."

"He's like that now," I said, feeling a surge of affection for my compassionate, gentle father.

"In my last term at university," Izzie continued, "where I was reading English literature, I fell in love.

"Despite the distractions I managed to get my degree." Izzie sighed. "But when I introduced Jake to my parents they took against him.

"I loved him desperately and I was furious they wouldn't give him a chance. So, being me, I rebelled, ran off and married him anyway."

"Oh, Izzie," I breathed. "What happened?"

"It only lasted a few months. After promising me the earth, he didn't come home one day." Izzie gave me a rueful smile.

"I never saw him again. I was heartbroken, Tasha, and mortified that my parents had been right.

"But they had no sympathy. All they showed was disdain and said they'd told me so."

"Oh, Izzie," I said again. "So what did you do?"

"We had an awful row and I left," Izzie said. "I ended up in Raston. Fortunately I had a little money. I'd written articles, and had a short story or two published even whilst I was studying.

"I booked in at a B and B whilst I looked for a job. I was willing to do anything." Izzie gazed into her glass for a moment. "I ended up in this very cottage as housekeeper to a retired police detective who lived here.

"I was surly, hurt and angry, but somehow he got through to me. We became great friends. He encouraged me to continue with my articles and newspaper columns where I could." Izzie sighed.

"The stories he told me are what inspired me to write my crime thrillers. And when he died the dear man left me his cottage."

"So that's when R.I. Derekson was born," I breathed. "What an incredible story.

"But why did you never want to have any contact with Dad?" I asked her, feeling, despite myself, rather hurt.

Izzie was silent for a while.

"You have to understand what my life became, Tasha," she said eventually. "I was bitterly hurt at how Jake and my parents had treated me. I wanted no contact with anyone from my old life.

"Over time I grew into the proverbial loner, happy with my own company and my writing. Until I met Hal. And you, Tasha. You've become very dear to me."

"Oh, Izzie," I said, squeezing her hand. "Dad will be so pleased how things have turned out for you."

"I'm sorry we've been out of touch for so long. Hurt pride has a lot to answer for, Tasha." She sighed.

* * * *

After a year in which Dad and I grew ever closer to Izzie and Hal, we travelled down to the Yorkshire moors to see them married.

Apart from Hal's best man, Dad and I were the only guests, just as Izzie wanted it. I cried happy tears as I watched them lovingly exchange their vows in her sweetly scented walled garden.

Apart from Hal, Dad and me, Izzie guards her privacy ferociously. Fortunately Hal says that, with all the people he meets in his line of work, he's happy to be a loner with Izzie when he comes home.

When Dad first told me about his sister, all alone in the world with not a friend to care for her, I'd privately christened her "poor aunt Izzie".

But I can now rejoice in how her story had evolves into such an abundantly rich and rewarding one.

And how blessed I feel that we have found her again. ■

Curtain Call

by Eirin Thompson

GLORIA looked at the curtains and sighed.

"What's up?" Hugh asked, lifting his nose from his newspaper.

"It's these," Gloria began. "They've done their job, but they're starting to fray round the edges, and the hems are looking worn. We need to replace them."

"OK. So we'll get new curtains, but why the sad face?"

"You'd only say I was being sentimental if I told you."

"Try me."

"We had these curtains made nearly thirty years ago," Gloria explained. "When the kids were all still small."

"They cost us four hundred pounds – which was a huge amount of money, but this is such a big window."

"I remember. When the chap came to hang them, he said we had actually chosen an upholstery fabric – hence the price. No-one had pointed that out when we were ordering them, though."

"It is a really heavy cloth," Gloria replied. "That's why they've lasted so long."

"But none of this explains why you're looking sad," Hugh pointed out. "I thought women liked getting new things for the house."

"Not this woman," Gloria answered. "We got those curtains when we did up the room one Christmas. I remember the fairy lights making the lovely red and gold of the fabric glow.

"It was the year Ollie got his Tracy Island and Jack had his Scalextric set up at the other end of the room. The girls were in their bouncy chairs watching the tree lights twinkle.

"Those curtains have been with us every day since then," she finished sadly.

Hugh nodded thoughtfully.

"They've seen some service, all right."

"They have indeed. They've dictated every bit of furnishing and decorating we've done in here since we got them. Everything was chosen to go with the curtains."

"I remember Tilly running up them when she was a kitten," Hugh said with a chuckle.

"I don't recall you laughing about that particular party trick at the time," Gloria reminded him. "What about Gemma and Chloe always hiding behind them for hide-and-seek? They've been part of the fabric of our family for so long."

"I'll pour us each a glass of wine and we'll drink a toast to the old curtains and their years of sterling service," Hugh suggested with a grin.

"Then we'll talk about giving the room a completely new look," he added. "It might be fun."

*　　*　　*　　*

Gloria knew that all of their four children liked coming back to the old place.

They loved the log fires in chilly weather, sprawling on the big, comfy sofas and flicking through the family photograph albums to see themselves as youngsters.

Illustration by Shutterstock.

News of a sitting-room make-over might not be welcome, she suspected.

Sure enough, when she mentioned it to Chloe and Gemma, they were horrified.

"But we love this room!" they cried.

"Look at these," Gloria said, showing them the damage on the curtains. "I've turned a blind eye for quite a while, but they're really tatty. We have to replace them."

"Ollie won't be happy," Chloe warned. "You know how much he hates change."

Jack was stricken, too.

"Why do people always think new is better?" he asked with a huge sigh. "But if it's what you really want, I'll help with the papering and painting, if you like."

As the oldest, Ollie had the most memories.

He didn't complain at all, though – he just nodded silently, as if he had been given some very bad news about a beloved pet. Gloria found that the hardest of all.

* * * *

In the end, all four kids mucked in with the make-over. Gloria and Hugh had decided on a soft blue palette. There was new wallpaper and paint, new wall lights, and made-to-measure covers for the sofas and armchair.

Instead of curtains, they'd gone for stylish blinds plus wooden shutters.

"It looks fab," Gloria commented when the new plants had been placed and the cushions and throws added.

"Very relaxing," Hugh added, standing in the doorway to survey their efforts.

"What will you do with the old things?" Ollie enquired.

"I've given the cushion covers, the rug and the lampshades to the charity shop," Gloria informed them.

"And the curtains?" Ollie asked.

"I was coming to that." Gloria smiled.

"Shall I do the honours?" Hugh proposed.

"You'll need a hand," Gloria commented. "Guys, sit down. Your father and I will be a minute."

* * * *

"Ta-da!" Gloria and Hugh plonked four footstools down on the new rug.

"What are these?" Gemma asked.

"Your dad and I found an evening class that started just after New Year," Gloria explained. "Upholstery for beginners.

"We took along the old curtains and made you each a footstool from the centre of the fabric, which was still in good condition."

"It was a lot of fun," Hugh added. "We weren't the fastest students in the class, but we got there in the end."

"Now you each have a little memento of the red and gold curtains for your own homes." Gloria grinned. "What do you think?"

"I think we have a very clever mum and dad," Chloe answered.

"And very talented, too," Gemma added.

Jack lifted one of the stools and turned it over.

"Nice workmanship, you two. And a very nice thought, as well."

Ollie was smiling.

"I love it. Thank you," he said.

Much later, after all the young people had gone, Gloria and Hugh were relaxing on the sofa, their feet up on the ottoman.

"You try to look after them the best you can while they're at home, and then send them out into the world and cross your fingers that they're all right," Gloria said, her head on Hugh's shoulder.

Hugh seemed to think for a moment before answering.

"Are we talking about the kids or the footstools?" he asked. ■

Vintage Cleaning Tips from the "Friend"

Ammonia

A PRODUCT of the nitrogen that occurs naturally in plants and animals, ammonia has been used for washing and dyeing cloth as well as in the tanning industry since Classical times. It was also used to remove rust from iron. The process of extracting and converting nitrogen present in the air was developed in the early twentieth century, making household ammonia more available.

"Friend" readers were quick to take advantage.

In 1921, spring-cleaning hints suggested, "Windows should be cleaned with whiting, mixed with a little ammonia, and polished with a soft rag". If your brasswork was tarnished, "a very good reviver can be made as follows: Dissolve some mottled scouring soup with a little ammonia, apply with a soft brush, and after a short time rub well with a rag. There will be a brilliant polish, which can be varnished over with transparent varnish, and the article will keep bright for a very long time."

One intrepid reader shared the following recipe for homemade metal polish in 1940: "A simple metal polish consists of equal parts of full-strength ammonia and olive oil. This polish has no sediment and removes obstinate tarnish with little trouble. It will also remove old, dry sediment left in the crevices of embossed or engraved metal by other mixtures. It can be used, also, for copper and silver." Powerful stuff – but not something to repeat if you value your nasal passages!

It could also be used to banish moths from carpets, but the method suggested in 1957 looks pretty labour intensive!

"Put a quarter of a pound of rock ammonia into a pail and add half a gallon of boiling water. Soak a piece of flannel in the pail. Wring it and lay it flat on the carpet, then iron with a very hot iron until it is dry. Treat the whole carpet in this way and all the moths' eggs will be destroyed."

Even diluted, ammonia can cause severe burns and damage to lungs, so always use with caution and never mix with any detergent or cleaner that contains bleach. ■

Secret Admirer

by Susan Wright

A FTER she'd put the card back in its envelope, Michelle crept up the stairs and tapped on her daughter's door.

"What time is it?" Megan muttered. "What do you want, Mum?"

"You've got a card," Michelle whispered as she walked into the room and flicked on the light.

"A card?" Megan repeated, screwing up her eyes against the brightness. "What sort of card?"

"A Valentine's card." Michelle sat down on her daughter's bed and handed her the envelope. "Somebody put it through the letter-box. It's lovely. It has a big red heart on the front."

Megan frowned.

"How do you know that?"

"Because I opened it," Michelle admitted sheepishly. "I'm sorry, Megan, but it was on the doormat when I went downstairs and I thought it was for me."

"For you?" Megan said, sounding as if she'd never heard anything so ridiculous in her life.

"I thought your dad might have come over all romantic," Michelle replied. "And it is addressed to M. Henderson, so it could have been for me."

Megan frowned again as she stared at the envelope.

"It might be for you. I can't think of anybody who would have sent me a card." She grinned. "Maybe you have a secret admirer, Mum."

"I doubt that," Michelle returned.

"But you must have," Megan argued, looking at the card more carefully. "That isn't Dad's writing on the envelope, is it? Hasn't anybody written inside?"

Michelle shook her head.

"No, you don't write inside Valentine's cards."

"Some people do," Megan pointed out. "This person obviously wanted

Illustration by Shutterstock.

to be mysterious.

"It looks like a woman's writing on the envelope to me."

"Does it?" Michelle frowned.

"Yes, it's all flowery," Megan replied, her eyes twinkling as she opened the envelope and took out the card. "So your secret admirer must be a woman.

"She must be quite a wealthy woman, too, because this is a very expensive card!" she added.

"I know," Michelle replied. "I really can't imagine that it's for me, though, Megan. "It must be from somebody at college."

"But there isn't anyone," Megan insisted. "There are a few guys I like, but they're not interested in me, and the only one who likes me wouldn't dream of buying a card like this."

"Why not?" Michelle asked.

"Because he's not the sort."

Megan opened the card and read the short romantic verse inside.

"Gareth's a geek, and I shouldn't imagine he's even heard of Valentine's Day."

Michelle laughed.

"Oh, I'm sure he would have heard of it."

"Yeah, but he wouldn't spend money on a card for me," Megan insisted. "Plus, he doesn't know where I live so he couldn't have delivered it."

"Perhaps he asked one of your friends where you live," Michelle suggested.

"They would have told me if he had," Megan reasoned, running her fingers over the red heart.

"Gareth wouldn't be up this early on a Tuesday morning anyway. He usually plays computer games for most of the night and gets up really late."

"Maybe he delivered it last night," Michelle suggested. "It wasn't there when I went to bed, so I assumed that somebody had delivered it this morning, but I suppose they could have delivered it in the middle of the night."

"Yes, they could have," Megan acknowledged. "I'm sure it can't be for me, though.

"Dad must have bought it for you and asked somebody else to write the envelope. Have you been throwing out any hints about Valentine's Day?"

Michelle shook her head.

"I gave up on all that years ago. You know what your dad's like. He thinks these special days are just a big con."

"Maybe he felt guilty," Megan suggested, handing the card and envelope back to her mum. "Maybe somebody had a go at him and said he ought to appreciate you more."

Michelle frowned.

"Like who?"

"Oh, I don't know," Megan muttered, the tone of her voice indicating that she'd had enough of the conversation and wanted to go back to sleep. "Why don't you ask him?"

"He's asleep," Michelle told her.

"So?" Megan cried. "I was asleep, but that didn't stop you coming in here!"

"No, but your dad gets irritable if I wake him up."

"So you'll just have to ask him later," Megan reasoned.

Suddenly they both heard the sound of somebody shutting the bathroom door.

"Unless that's him," Megan added.

Michelle stood up, walked to her bedroom and came back.

"No, your dad's still asleep, so it's your grandad in the bathroom."

"Oh, well," Megan said, as she snuggled down in her bed. "You'll just have to think about something else until Dad gets up then."

"Yes, I suppose I will," Michelle agreed, turning to go.

But then Megan sat up suddenly.

"Unless . . ."

"Unless what?"

"Unless the card's for Grandad!" Megan exclaimed. "He doesn't have a

Escape

Perhaps you'd like to run away
Or spread your wings and fly,
Or maybe find a sunny spot
To let the world go by.
Perhaps you'd like a golden beach
Or sail a turquoise sea,
Or maybe on a mountain top
You'd set your spirit free.

It isn't easy to escape,
We all have things to do,
We all have people we must see –
Perhaps they need us, too.
But in our minds and in our thoughts
These places we can find,
Just close your eyes and drift away
And leave the world behind.

So just for now forget the news,
Forget about the weather,
Relax with me a little while
And we'll escape together!

Iris Hesselden.

Shutterstock.

secret admirer, does he?"

Michelle shook her head.

"Of course he hasn't."

"Are you sure?"

"Well, no, I'm not sure," Michelle admitted, wondering if her father-in-law had met anybody at his bridge club that he hadn't told her about. "But I don't think he has, and anyway, his name doesn't begin with M, does it?"

"No." Megan looked momentarily downcast. "But maybe the M is supposed to be Mr!"

Michelle looked down at the envelope.

"Yes, you could be right, actually. I thought there was a little flick on the right side of the M, but looking again, it could be that it's supposed to be Mr."

Megan grinned.

"So who has Grandad met?"

"I've no idea," Michelle said slowly as the bathroom door opened and her father-in-law shuffled out.

"Hey, Bill, were you expecting a Valentine's card?" she called out.

Bill looked at her curiously.

"No – why?"

"Well, somebody's delivered one and we think it must be for you," Michelle told him, handing him the envelope. "And we don't recognise the writing. Do you?"

Bill peered at the envelope and turned bright red.

"Yes, I do, actually."

"And?" Michelle stared at him.

Bill couldn't take his eyes off the envelope, turning it over and over in his hands.

"It's Avril's writing," he explained finally.

"Avril?" Michelle repeated, wondering why he'd never mentioned a woman with that name.

"And who might Avril be?" Megan demanded, all thoughts of sleep forgotten. "And why have we never met her – or even heard about her before this?"

Bill grinned at his granddaughter.

"Well, I thought she was just a friend," he replied happily, "but it looks as if I was wrong, doesn't it?"

"It does," Michelle agreed.

Bill smiled at her, then looked a bit worried.

"You don't think Stuart will be upset if he finds out I've got myself a girlfriend? I wouldn't want him to think I was trying to replace his mother or anything like that."

"Of course he won't think anything of the kind," Megan said stoutly. "Will he, Mum?"

"No, I'm sure he'll be fine about it," Michelle assured him, remembering how devastated her husband had been when his mother had died.

"It's been a long time, Bill, and Stuart wants you to be happy. And by the look of things you are – am I right?"

Bill's face took on a puckish expression.

"Maybe you are," he agreed. He looked down at the card again. "This has certainly cheered up my day.

"Well, ladies, if you'll excuse me, I think I'll have a shower and a shave, then nip along to the shops for some nice chocolates.

"I might pay Avril a surprise visit and see if she fancies going out for lunch."

He sauntered across the landing to the bathroom. As he closed the door, they could hear him singing.

Megan and Michelle looked at each other and laughed.

"Well, now that the mystery is solved," Megan said, "do you mind if I go back to sleep?" ■

Schiehallion, Perthshire

Perthshire's most famous mountain offers stunning views for those fit enough to scale this 3,553 ft Munro. The uphill climb rewards you, on a clear day, with a picture-perfect setting, with Loch Rannoch at its foot. However, as with any mountain, you should be on your guard for any sudden change in weather.

Legends and myths abound around the "fairy hill of the Caledonians", with the Blue Witch being just one of them. She has the power to whip up blustery weather in no time.

Another is that some folk mistakenly believe Schiehallion to be an extinct volcano, but its conical shape was formed during the ice ages. It was this very shape that attracted a science experiment that aimed to use the mountain to calculate the weight of the world. That was back in 1774, and Reverend Nevil Maskelyne, Britain's Astronomer Royal, also enlisted the help of mathematician Charles Hutton. Through this project, contour lines on maps came about.

The habitat is home to mountain hare, ptarmigan and deer, with golden eagles to be seen circling above. Interesting flora and fauna can also be found here. Over 2,150 acres of East Schiehallion is managed by the John Muir Trust.

Feast Of Fools

by H. Johnson-Mack

HELOISE DU BOIS studied her reflection in the polished bowl. Folk said she had a fair face, but as she was doomed only to view herself in a distorted image, she preferred to reserve judgement.

Besides, being an heiress to a fine manor set in fertile land meant it didn't much matter how she looked; she would be courted for her wealth alone.

Sighing, she twitched smooth a fold of her gown. Tonight, her uncle would host a raucous Feast of Fools, the traditional evening festivities on the first day of April.

She wasn't looking forward to it, even with a new draped-sleeve dress and glittering bronze girdle to wear. The April Fools' world was traditionally turned on its head – nothing was what it seemed.

It was a bright morning, the welcome scent of spring in the air after a long, cold winter. Heloise couldn't help smiling as she headed through the busy bailey of her Uncle Amien's keep to the stables.

Bramwich was a handsome demesne, set in verdant, undulating lands. But then everything looked so much better in the sunshine.

Her smile faded as she heard the peremptory voice of her cousin calling her.

"Where are you running off to?" Margery demanded.

"For a ride."

"You'll have to wait. Papa wants you."

Stifling a sigh, Heloise headed back within. She appreciated her uncle adopting her as his ward after her papa had fallen in battle and her mama remarried, with new stepchildren to raise, especially as Amien's only child was absurdly jealous of Heloise.

It couldn't be easy for him, dealing with two marriageable maids in his household. But she wished he wouldn't try quite so hard to find her a husband.

His latest candidate was younger than the last, but to Heloise he was too mercenary and with a dangerous glint in his dark, sharp gaze.

Richard Wariner seemed to have no time for women, especially her. She felt as though he looked right through her, into her soul, and didn't

Illustration by Mandy Dixon.

necessarily approve.

Like now, she reflected, when she saw him standing with her uncle by the hall's huge hearth.

"Good morrow, my dear." Amien greeted her with a smile. "How are preparations coming along?"

"Very well, Uncle," Heloise replied with a polite bob. "The cooks and entertainers are determined to keep up your tradition of a wonderful Feast of Fools."

"Splendid!" Amien tapped his ample stomach in satisfaction then slanted a glance Wariner's way. "Er . . . Sir Richard has yet to see the West Ridge, so I thought you might like to escort him."

Heloise executed another, lower curtsey.

"Of course. If you'd care to follow me, sir . . ."

She led the way to the stables, only once glancing behind. Wariner was a silent shadow, seemingly unimpressed with Amien's plans for his entertainment, and she swallowed as she motioned to the groom to saddle Amien's sleek courser for the dark knight and her own grey mare.

"'Tis a lovely morning for seeing the ridge," she ventured as they trotted over the drawbridge and out into the countryside.

His dark eyes flashed with wry humour.

"There is no need for pleasantries, my lady. You wish for this outing – and our betrothal – as little as I."

Heloise lifted her chin.

"Well, if bluntness is to be the order of the day, then I need not tarry here just to be polite. And by the way, whatever you think of me, sir, it can be no worse than my opinion of you."

Spurring her horse, she broke into a fast trot then a satisfying gallop.

Having soon left Wariner behind, Heloise gave herself up to the joy of riding fast and free through reawakening fields and forest.

When her mare began breathing too heavily, she slowed and trotted through the meadows, stroking the horse's neck, before turning home.

Their peace was short-lived, though this rider was more welcome to Heloise than her last. She reined in as a whipcord-slim gentleman approached from the direction of the river.

"Well met, my lady." Conrad Valentine greeted her with a doff of his embroidered cap. "May I escort you back to the keep?"

His unnecessary gallantry made her smile.

"That would be kind."

"I am looking forward to the festivities," Valentine said. "Your uncle's feasts are famous."

Heloise acknowledged this with a nod, instinctively comparing his easy conversational manner with the gritty silence of Sir Richard. How frustrating, then, that it was to Richard her uncle was determined to wed her.

Conrad Valentine's family had not the prestige of the Wariners, but his charm and dancing blue eyes were much more popular with the females of Bramwich.

Valentine's most assiduous admirer was almost certainly Margery, and whatever plans Amien had for both girls' futures, he wasn't noticeably discouraging Heloise from spending time with this man.

Though not one to show her feelings, Heloise would have welcomed her cousin's companionship, having no close female friends unless she counted her maid Eda, who'd been with her since childhood.

But the older girl had resented her from the start and unfortunately Valentine's obvious attention was just another spark that would fuel Margery's fire of dislike.

"Is all well, my lady?" Valentine asked, startling Heloise out of her gloomy thoughts. "You seem a little distracted."

She offered him a smile.

"Just reflecting on this lovely morning, and the arrival of spring."

Valentine gave a dramatic sigh.

"'Tis beautiful, is it not? You should see Normandy at this time of year; the sun is positively golden."

Something stirred in Heloise's memory – something Amien had told her.

"Sir Richard was knighted in Normandy, I believe."

Valentine grimaced.

"Aye, lady, for his sins." He paused then added, "Mayhap I should not speak so in present company, but not every man who wins his spurs is all a knight should traditionally be."

Heloise's hands tightening on the reins made her mare start.

"If you know aught sinful of Sir Richard, sir, you should speak of it to my uncle."

Valentine looked alarmed.

"Forgive me, my lady," he said quickly. "I did not mean to upset you. Richard Wariner is an experienced, skilful fighter of whom his noble patron is very fond."

Which, Heloise reflected wryly, very neatly confirmed nothing at all.

The beautiful blue skies soon faded to grey. It was a mirror of Heloise's mood as the day dissolved into her acting as mediator in the kitchens, where pressures over the forthcoming feast finally exploded, then avoiding her uncle and his blunt hints on her future.

"You will have to make a decision soon," he told her as they took their places on the dais for the evening meal.

Margery shot her a malevolent look and Heloise sighed. With her cousin and the man Amien intended as her betrothed quite obvious about their apathy towards her, it was a balm to see the warm smile of Conrad Valentine as he took a seat further down the table.

Margery's mood instantly revived when the jesters her papa had hired for the celebrations came dancing in to the lively beat of shawm and drum.

The elder girl became quite pretty as her delight in the arrivals animated her features.

Clapping her hands, she gave a gasp as a little woman swathed in black swirled to a halt before her and flourished a beribboned marotte, its hanging bells tinkling and gleaming.

"What will fortune bring this pretty lady before the Feast of Fools?" Grinning, the woman traced the lines on Margery's palm with the jester stick. "I see love in your future, and it will transform your life."

Margery beamed, and the little woman curtsied and whirled away, stopping abruptly when she saw Heloise.

The pleasure drained from her wizened features. She lowered the marotte.

"Beware," she murmured in a warning note quite unlike her previous merry tone. "Beware the shadows, for therein lies the way to an early grave."

She was swept up in the rest of the entertainers dancing past the dais at that moment, and whatever else she had intended to say was lost.

Heloise swallowed, stunned into silence.

Margery's buoyant mood continued, especially when she danced first with both of Heloise's supposed courtiers. Heloise escaped as soon as she could, her own senses strangely morose. It was as if the fortune teller had cast a cloud over her.

She was immediately aware of a change when she returned to the hall, now half empty, which was quickly explained by one of the maids.

"A fire has broken out, my lady, in one of the barns."

Heloise hurried outside, her breath catching at the sight of a small but sinister lick of flames up the side of a grain storage barn.

A crowd was gathered there; some folk were merely spectating whilst others helped to douse the growing flames.

"Is anyone inside?" a voice cried, and someone replied, "My lady Heloise was seen going in there."

Heloise's heart leapt into her throat as a terrifying thought occurred to her.

"Oh, sweet heaven! Eda!"

She ran towards the open door, striking out blindly when a rock-solid arm snaked round her and held her back.

"Let me go! My maid is in there!"

"Easy," Wariner's voice said in her ear. "She is safe."

As Heloise looked wildly up at him, he nodded to a figure lying some yards away, being comforted by one of the cooks.

"Why would anyone believe your maid was you?" he demanded.

"I gave her one of my gowns," Heloise replied distractedly. "The yellow laced bodice is a favourite of hers."

Wariner's brows rose.

"You are very generous, madam."

"My uncle bought me a new one for the feast, so I could easily afford to."

He eyed her inscrutably for a long moment.

"So not such an ice queen after all," he murmured.

Heloise, unnerved by his comment and the effect his gaze was having on her, pulled out of his hold and hurried over to her maid.

To her immense relief, Eda had escaped with little more than scraped skin and shock. Heloise directed a couple of strong men to carry the maid to her chamber.

"Lady Heloise! Are you all right? They were saying you were in the barn . . ."

"I am fine," she reassured Valentine, instinctively grasping his arms as he sagged. "It was a mistake."

"Thank heaven for that!" He laid a hand over hers. "I could not bear it if something happened to you."

Heloise caught her breath as he leaned towards her as though about to steal a kiss. At the last moment, he drew back, mumbled something she couldn't catch, then hurried off.

Before she could examine her feelings about this, her cousin materialised before her, bristling with barely stifled anger. She cast a sharp glance behind her at the retreating Valentine.

"Watch your step, cousin," she warned.

Then, gathering up her skirts in tight fists, she stalked away.

* * * *

The first day of April was bright and pleasantly warm, which augured well for the new season. Heloise, however, was still dogged by the smoky shadows of the previous night.

Eda had suffered no ill effects from her adventure, reporting that it had been mere moments after she'd stepped inside the barn in search of her latest fancy (a rather shy kennelman) when she heard noises outside and saw the first lick of flame.

Though the door had jammed, she knew there was another way out, and it was only after she'd squeezed through into fresh air that the "what might have been" had made her come over faint.

Her next words now had the same effect on Heloise.

"That fortune teller was right."

A finger of fear crept up to encircle Heloise's throat.

"What mean you?"

"Someone believed I was you, that's what I mean," Eda said ominously. "And I doubt that spark of fire that could have burned the whole barn – and anyone inside – was a mere coincidence.

"I'm worried, my lady. I believe you are in danger."

Heloise swallowed. The memory of Wariner's eyes staring into hers, then Margery watching her like a hawk, stiffened her spine.

She was a Du Bois. She would not be cowed by intimidation and shadows . . .

*   *   *   *

Heloise spent the day assisting her uncle with festivity preparations, suffering his blatant hints on her betrothal in silence. He'd certainly lived up to his reputation, she admitted, when she returned suitably gowned and girdled that evening.

The hall was garlanded with fresh seasonal foliage, firelight and wall sconces blazing with bright light that reflected off the shiny bells of the chief jester, known tonight as the Lord of Misrule, dancing to the minstrels' merry music.

There was a general feeling of anticipated mischief as kitchen staff brought in trenchers and bowls full of steaming food with tummy-tugging smells, all served backwards as was the custom on this topsy-turvy night.

As the festivities progressed, Heloise, more watchful, was seeing double meaning in everything. Why were the minstrels repeatedly circling round her like crows on carrion?

Why did Margery seem to be watching her so closely? When Richard Wariner suddenly appeared at her elbow, she jumped, despite her resolve not to be intimidated.

"Will you have some wine, my lady?"

She glanced up. He was leaning over her, like a shield from the rowdy celebrations in the rest of the hall, and she was enfolded in a warm relief, feeling as though she were protected.

But that couldn't be; this was the man who barely tolerated her.

Yet here he was, offering her a goblet with the ghost of a smile.

When he looked directly into her eyes, the smile was replaced with his usual frown.

"What is it?" he asked gruffly.

She forced her chin up.

"I am fine, sir. Just a little giddy from all this heat."

"You will not dance with me, then?"

She shook her head.

Wariner hesitated, then stepped back.

"As you wish. Take care, my lady," he muttered before moving away.

Heloise dabbed at her throat with a small linen square, trying to stave off sudden faintness. The world turned upside down, indeed!

As she watched, the darkness beyond the candles and firelight seemed to stretch and lengthen, the dancers' spinning silhouettes apeing the appearance of giant, grasping eagle talons . . .

Unable to bear it any longer, Heloise rose and made her way through the crowd to the nearest exit, which happened to be the winding stairway up to the south tower roof, and out into some blessed fresh air.

Sighing in relief as she breathed deep, she stared up at the winking stars. As she'd scared off a crow roosting on the crenellations, she was now alone. But not for long.

When the stairway door opened, she instinctively reared back. It wasn't just the slithered silence of the shadowy figure's arrival, but the ominous feeling that came with it.

Then she saw the figure's face. It was Valentine's face, but not as she'd known it. Now it was transformed into a devil's mask, sinister and bitter.

"You're surprisingly troublesome," he said.

"You were supposed to have perished in an unfortunate fire, but thanks to your unexpected generosity, I got the wrong girl. An April Fool, indeed! Now it will have to be a tragic tumble off the tower."

Still reeling from the change in him, Heloise gazed wildly round the small rooftop as Valentine began to advance. There was nowhere to run.

She stiffened her spine. She wouldn't succumb without a fight . . .

"Cousin!"

Heloise whirled as Margery burst through the door, angry, determined and brandishing a dagger.

Heart in mouth, Heloise's hands shot out in self defence as, with a screeching battle cry, Margery launched herself at Valentine!

The unexpected attack took him totally off guard, and though she lost her weapon, Margery was able to propel him backwards. Heloise gasped as they grappled dangerously close to the gap between the crenellated stone edge.

She glanced round for something to aid her cousin and, finding nothing, ran to add her weight into the mix.

Valentine had succeeded in overcoming Margery's initial flight and now had her arm in a vice, bending her back against the edge.

Heloise tried to drag him off, earning a savage strike across the face that sent her spinning off balance.

Before she could fall, she was caught in strong, steadying arms and set upright. Wariner!

With a huge sigh of relief, Heloise watched Richard wrench Margery free of Valentine's grasp and twirl her back to safety. Then she screamed a warning as Valentine rushed at him from behind.

He turned just in time to deflect what could have been a deadly push, and it was Conrad Valentine himself who toppled over the edge.

* * * *

The body of Conrad Valentine had been exclaimed over and taken carefully to the chapel. The Feast of Fools festivities were tactfully wound down. Now the ladies of Bramwich could finally retire to their bed chambers to reflect over that dreadful rooftop scene.

"I don't know how to thank you for coming to my rescue," Heloise said, sitting tentatively beside Margery on the rug before a flickering hearth. "Though I thought for a moment that you'd come to assist him."

Margery sniffed and lowered her eyes.

"I cannot blame you. I've hardly been very welcoming since you were sent here. I am not naturally easy at relationships, especially with women, and you are so annoyingly lovely . . ." She offered Heloise a tentative smile.

"But I could try harder from now on, if you are willing."

Heloise threw her arms around her.

"I would love that! Tell me," she said as she drew back a little, "how did you know what Valentine was really like? I was under the impression you were sweet on him."

"I was at first," Margery admitted, "but the more I observed him, the more my feelings began to alter. An unguarded look, a clenched fist hidden behind a cloak and a charming smile . . .

"I found myself doubting and following him for all the wrong reasons. It was then that I discovered he had an unhealthy interest in you."

Heloise swallowed as a flashback of the tower top shuddered through her.

"How could I have been so blind to his true nature?"

Margery's expression was kindly.

"Mayhap you wanted to believe in his affection for you too much to let yourself see the truth."

Heloise looked away. She had been desperate for affection, yes, but from an entirely different direction.

*　　*　　*　　*

The candles had long since burned out and Margery lay sleeping, but for Heloise rest wouldn't come. She sat wrapped in a woollen coverlet by the quiet hearth, her thoughts furious and frustrated.

For all her proud manner, she had misjudged and mishandled everything.

When the tap-tap sounded on the chamber door, she swallowed and slowly rose, hardly daring to hope.

Drawing the door ajar, there stood Richard Wariner on the other side, his eyes, shadowed by the brazier he carried, impossible to read.

"You cannot sleep?" he asked on a murmur. When she shook her head, he extended his free hand. "Have you ever seen the dawn?"

The kitchen gardens lay still and silent in the first grey threads of morning. Heloise allowed Wariner to lead her through the walled gate to a tufted seat smelling of sweet chamomile.

"So, mistress," he began once they were side by side, a polite gap between them. "Why does sleep elude you?"

"Can you not guess?" Heloise whispered.

Wariner scowled, brushing her bruised cheek with a fingertip.

"Conrad Valentine does not deserve your distress or your pity. He would have killed any one or all three of us.

"Do you know why he came here? Why he deliberately set out to secure your affections?

"It was because I had been chosen for your husband, and he has been awaiting just such an opportunity to strike at me."

"But why?"

"Years ago, we were taught together as pages and knights, and Valentine could never accept that I was better at both than he was.

"His envy grew to hatred over time, which burst into flames when I won the love of the youngest daughter of the noble house we'd been fostered into."

"What happened?" Heloise prompted when he fell silent.

Wariner swallowed.

"She died, suddenly and under circumstances I've often wondered about. I believe it was no accident, and that Valentine was responsible.

"The trampling of my heart wasn't enough for him, though, and he vowed that I would never be happy if he could prevent it."

Heloise didn't realise her hand had crossed to cover his until he gripped her palm, raising it to study her slim fingers.

"I thought I could never love again," he murmured. "Until I saw you."

"You lie!" Heloise exclaimed. "You barely like me, and wanted our betrothal as little as I!"

"Have you ever been afraid of your feelings, of succumbing to something that could hurt you so much, you may not survive it?

"I believed you an ice maiden and tried to fight my fascination, especially when you seemed to favour Valentine's suit. But I could not keep my distance for long, and thank the saints for that!

"If not, I dread to think what could have happened on that rooftop, even with plucky Margery rushing to your aid.

"You do not speak, lady," he said after a heavy silence. "Have I ruined any chance of winning your heart?"

"You wondered why I could not sleep," Heloise replied softly, turning her gaze to the man anxiously watching her.

"Nor would you if you were cursing yourself for an April fool, and wishing with all you are that you could travel back in time and do things differently, to recognise the worth of one man and the witty lies of another.

"Then mayhap that worthy man would look at you differently, too, and propose to you because he wanted to and not because he felt obliged."

She gasped as Wariner pulled her roughly into his arms.

"Do you tell me you want me?" he demanded, laughing when she nodded. "The world does indeed turn upside down on the Feast of Fools!"

"Look, my lord." Heloise tipped her head towards the sky now streaked with gorgeous golden stripes.

"The new day dawns. 'Tis April Fools' no longer, but spring, the season of hope."

"And love, my lady fair." Wariner drew her head down, smiling into her eyes. "And love." ∎

Granny's
Household
Helpers

Vintage Cleaning Tips from the "Friend"

Chalk

LONG ago, ancient sea creatures lived their lives and died, settling finally into the ocean floor. Little did they know that, over aeons, the calcium they contained would transform into a brittle white rock. Some millennia later, new life forms would find all kinds of ingenious purposes for that rock, from building to writing on boards to transfer knowledge to cleaning their homes – and even their teeth (chalk is a common ingredient in toothpaste). Mildly abrasive and extremely absorbent, calcium carbonate, the chemical name for calcite or chalk, is useful around the home.

Book lovers in 1870 were given a handy tip to remove grease spots from their favourite tomes: "Scrape very fine some white chalk or whiting, and lay as much on the grease spot as will cover it (both on the top and under part of the leaf), get a moderately heated iron, and press it hard on the spot; by repeating this two or three times the paper will resume its original whiteness."

Marble fire surrounds were fashionable in Victorian times, so "Friend" readers must have been glad of the following 1885 recipe.

"To clean marble, the following is commended: Common soda, 2 pounds; powdered pumice-stone, 1 pound; finely-powdered chalk, 1 pound; pass through a fine sieve, and mix with water. Rub it well all over the marble, and the stains will be removed; then wash the marble over with soap and water, and it will be as clean as it was at first."

It came to the rescue for laundry, too. Battling mildew was as much a problem in 1904 as it is today, but help was at hand.

"Mildew will yield to neither hot nor cold water. It is the result of a fungus that requires killing, and only chemical action and sunshine combined can do this. A mixture of starch and soap, chalk and soap, or lemon juice and salt, or salts of lemon will be necessary. The articles must be laid in the sunshine and wetted from time to time with whatever remedy is adopted."

By the way, "salts of lemon" has nothing to do with lemons – more on this later! ■

Shutterstock.

A New
Dawn

by Lynda Franklin

ISA had planted the daffodil bulbs in September on a bright afternoon with a fresh breeze. She remembered thinking how lovely the garden would look when they flowered in the springtime.

She sat on the patio later that evening with James, drinking wine by candlelight as dusk slowly crept over the garden.

She couldn't remember how long they sat there – time didn't seem to matter much in those days.

After James left, the first few weeks were a blur. Lisa found her solace mainly in sleep and mindless daytime television, which distracted her mind.

She avoided phone calls from her parents and friends. She would get back to them all in time, but right now all she wanted – all she could cope with – was to be alone.

She needed time for her bruised heart to mend.

Early one morning, newly awake and watching light streaming through her bedroom window, Lisa found herself pulling on an old tracksuit, fleecy and somehow comforting.

Maybe her garden was the answer. James might not need her, but her garden did.

The paths were covered in autumn leaves and she began to sweep them clear, gathering up the bouquet of reds, yellows and browns into a small pile.

It was as if a dam was slowly being taken apart and her blood allowed to flow once more. With every invigorating movement she felt more energy return.

* * * *

November brought high winds and frosts, and by December the pond in Lisa's garden was covered in a thin layer of ice, and the beds dusted in snow.

Lisa wrapped up warmly at weekends and chipped away at the ice, smiling as she noticed snowdrops and winter pansies flowering beneath

Illustration by Shutterstock.

her apple tree.

The Saturday before Christmas an elderly man raised his hand from the garden next door.

"Hi!" Lisa called back in acknowledgement. "It's a bit chilly today."

"Certainly is." He took a step towards the fence. "I've had a bout of flu so I've not been out much."

"Nice to meet you. Have you been unwell, too?" he asked.

Lisa nodded. It was easier than explaining.

"I'm Lisa."

"George."

It was the start of a weekly conversation, usually about something fairly innocuous like the garden or the weather.

Over the course of several chats, Lisa learned that George was a widower and lived alone. She chose not to divulge anything much about her own life.

"Fancy a cup of tea?" George called from his back door on Christmas Eve.

Lisa looked up from her pottering and smiled at him.

"I'd like that. Thanks."

It felt strange knocking on the front door, dressed now in clean jeans and clutching a bottle of wine she had found at the back of the cupboard, but her nerves soon disappeared as George welcomed her in with a smile.

It was a small room, warm and cosy, and in the corner stood a little Christmas tree prettily decorated with bits of silver tinsel and coloured lights.

Lisa hadn't thought to put any decorations up at all, and had made excuses not to go to the office party.

She knew it wouldn't help, despite her friends insisting it would "get her out of herself".

In a moment of panic at the thought of facing people, she'd told her parents she was feeling under the weather and that she'd visit on Boxing Day if she felt better.

Christmas Day was the day she and James had been going to spend together for the first time. They'd planned it.

The thought of facing it by herself was daunting.

"I see you've brought wine," George said with a smile. "Shall we have a glass instead of tea?"

"Why not?" Lisa said.

So they shared the pleasant Chardonnay and Lisa decided she wouldn't think about James or what they might have been doing this Christmas.

"You work hard in your garden," George observed.

Lisa nodded.

"I love being in the garden. It helps."

George didn't ask why or what it helped. He didn't question her at all, but, most unexpectedly, Lisa found herself telling him anyway.

When she finished, he just nodded.

"It's not easy being on your own." He pointed to a photograph over the fire. "That's my Mary."

Mary was dressed in her best clothes and smiling.

"It was taken at a wedding," he added. "It's a nice one of her."

"You must miss her." Lisa replied, imagining her in this room, tidying up or passing George a cup of tea.

He nodded ruefully.

"She died two years ago."

Lisa expressed her condolences.

"And who is this?" There was another photo on the mantelpiece of a much younger man and woman smiling into the lens. "Is that you and Mary, too?"

George laughed.

"That's my son and his wife. They live in Australia. He's been there a long time now.

"I miss them, but you can't stand in their way, can you? You can't tie them to you."

"I suppose not." Lisa nodded.

"He's happy, and that's the main thing. He has a lovely wife and three children. I haven't met my grandchildren yet." George chuckled. "This wine's making me talk too much."

"Not as much as me!" Lisa laughed. "And I think it's about time we had a chance to talk."

"Well, let me just say one more thing," George went on. "If there's one thing I've learned over the years, it's that we don't always get a choice about what life throws at us, but we do get a choice about how we deal with it."

Lisa took a sip of wine to avoid answering.

His words were so absolutely true and so kindly meant that she was afraid she might cry.

* * * *

Christmas came and went, and January blustered in with cold winds and long days.

Lisa didn't go out in the garden so much, with the shorter days and inclement weather, but she always made time to meet George for a chat once a week.

It was becoming part of her weekend routine now, and she had to admit she was growing fond of her elderly neighbour.

He often talked to her about his life with Mary, but Lisa still never spoke about James.

"Lisa!"

It was late one afternoon and George's voice sounded agitated, louder than normal.

"You OK, George?" Lisa looked up from filling her bird feeder, squinting in the March sunshine.

"No. Well, yes, I'm fine." He walked over to the fence. "I've had an e-mail from Richard."

Lisa smiled.

"I didn't know you were into technology, George."

"You have to keep up if you can. Richard's coming home!"

"That's brilliant!" Lisa exclaimed. "How long's he coming for? I'd love to meet him."

George shook his head, trying to get his words out.

"He's been made redundant and they've decided to use the redundancy money to come home. Richard thinks he'll stand a better chance of getting a job here."

"But that's wonderful, George. You'll finally get to know your grandchildren."

"Yes." He seemed dazed by the whole situation. "I never expected it, Lisa. I never looked for this to happen.

"Yes, this is good for me, but I'd rather things had worked out for them."

Lisa smiled sympathetically.

"Of course you would, I know that. But it's just the way things have turned out. And you deserve it, George. You're a good man."

"I don't know about that. I just do the best I can." George smiled softly. "Mary was a great believer in that."

"A wise woman." Lisa nodded.

"Well, anyway, it looks like all your efforts are about to be rewarded," he went on.

"What do you mean?" Lisa asked, puzzled.

Springtime Smiles

Look – the little lambs!
It's springtime once more;
They leap and frisk in their black socks
And new terrain explore.
On the moors with Mum close by,
Sheep scattered far and wide,
New lambs, happy, full of life
Upon the green hillside.
And, of course, the little rabbits,
These mascots of the spring,
The gentle wild creatures
And all the joy they bring.
And yet, it seems, when we appear
They do not want to stay!
But we're grateful for the creatures
We came across today.

Dorothy McGregor.

"Haven't you noticed?"

George pointed at the bed Lisa had planted so carefully with daffodil bulbs in September.

Back then she had imagined the garden exploding with colour in the spring, a beautiful spread of gold and yellow.

"It will be like growing my own sunshine," she'd told James, and he'd laughed at her.

Thinking back, it hadn't been a nice laugh. He never did understand her love of the garden.

Now she could see little green shoots beginning to poke out of the dark wet earth, and there in the middle, all on its own, stood one glorious golden daffodil.

It swayed gently in the spring air, standing tall, rightly proud of being the first one to open up to the world.

"My daffodils," she breathed. "They're coming out!"

George chuckled.

"Looks like you've done a good job there."

Lisa wasn't sure why she felt so emotional looking at her daffodil, but somehow she felt connected to this little flower, planted in hope months ago.

Through all her sad times, she realised, throughout this long winter, this little bulb had lain dormant in the dark, waiting for the moment it could rise up and shine.

This little flower knew all it had to do was wait and the dawn would come. Didn't the dawn always follow the darkness?

"James didn't like daffodils much." She had said his name out loud.

George shrugged.

"Well, I think they'll look a treat."

"Yes, I think they will, too. A few more days and my garden will be a sea of yellow." Lisa looked up at George and smiled. "New life, that's what spring's all about, isn't it?"

George nodded.

"It certainly is. Mary always said springtime was the time for new beginnings. Mind you, it often meant she wanted me to paint the lounge!"

He looked carefully at Lisa and spoke more softly.

"Of course, you have to be ready for a new beginning."

Lisa smiled, looking down at her muddy hands.

"George, we need to celebrate. I'm going to wash up and then we'll break open the wine.

"It's not every day your son and family come home." She took a breath. "And I think that I'm finally ready for that new beginning, too."

"That's good to hear." George patted her on the shoulder and turned to go back indoors, chuckling to himself.

"You bring the bottle!"

Lisa pulled off her hat and shook her head, enjoying the feel of the fresh breeze ruffling her hair.

She bent down to look more closely at the little green shoots pushing their way towards the light.

"We'll grow together," she whispered to them, knowing how James would ridicule her if he could hear her.

But it didn't matter at all now what James thought.

Her little daffodil bulbs would push through the darkness that had been holding them for so long, get stronger day by day, and eventually rise up and shine as bright and golden as the sun.

And Lisa was determined that she would be right there beside them. ■

Paisley, Renfrewshire

This Scottish town is famous for many things, not least of all the "Jewel in Paisley's Crown" and one of its most prominent landmarks – the spectacular abbey, the origins of which date back to the 12th century. Among its beautiful stained-glass windows is the Wallace Memorial Window, celebrating the Scottish hero William Wallace, who was born in Elderslie, and reputedly educated by the monks of Paisley Abbey.

The abbey is one of many listed buildings in the town, which has the textile industry woven into its history, and you'll find a statue to Robert Tannahill, known as the "weaver poet", who began his working life as a hand-loom weaver at the age of just twelve.

The self-taught poet – who founded the world's oldest constituted Burns Club – lived in a cottage close to a spot infamous in the town's dark history, with tales of witchcraft remembered to this day. It's where the so-called "Bargarran witches" met their fate at the town's Gallow Green in 1697.

Easter Eggstravaganza

by Jan Snook

ELLIE would usually have been delighted to be sent out to mingle with the visitors at the theme park on such a beautiful spring day. Anything was better than being stuck in the office with her grim-faced boss, Dorothy Cullins – Miss Cullins to anyone as lowly as Ellie was.

Ellie didn't understand why anyone who appeared to dislike most of the human race, and who particularly loathed children, would choose to work in the public relations department of a theme park in any case.

"You're to circulate throughout the park, handing out chocolate eggs, apparently," Miss Cullins said with a sniff, making her disapproval of such uncalled-for generosity abundantly clear.

Ellie jumped eagerly to her feet.

"Are those the eggs?" she asked, seeing several cartons by the door next to a beribboned basket.

Without waiting for an answer, she opened the nearest carton and began to decant the brightly coloured eggs.

"Aren't you going to change first?" Miss Cullins asked sourly.

"Change?"

"Obviously!" Miss Cullins indicated another larger carton by her desk.

Ellie opened it in trepidation. The truth was dawning on her, and was confirmed when she saw the familiar furry stripes filling the box.

Her heart sank.

"What were you expecting?" her boss said triumphantly. "The paying public want to see Wally, not you. So hurry up and get into the costume."

Wally the Wabbit – the popular cartoon character on whom the theme park was based – was a giant striped purple, orange and dazzling lime green rabbit. He was also very fat and wore bright red wellies and sunglasses, the kaleidoscope lenses of which spun round like whirligigs.

Ellie lifted the costume out of the box. There were vast cushions that had to be strapped on before she could step into it. Then there was the enormous plastic head, which she had to jam on her own head.

It had been made for someone a foot taller and much wider than Ellie (even after the cushions), and the wellies were like boats.

Illustration by André Leonard.

She wasn't sure she'd even be able to get down the stairs in it.

"Don't forget this," Miss Cullins said, handing her the huge blue and yellow umbrella that Wally habitually carried.

"I'll boil in this," Ellie grumbled. "Seriously, I think I might pass out."

Miss Cullins shrugged, but looked happier than Ellie had ever seen her.

"There's a button on the glasses that you push to make the lenses spin," Miss Cullins informed her, "so make sure you use it!

"And don't come back until everyone in the park has had an egg. Only one each, remember. And mind you don't eat any yourself."

How? How did Miss Cullins think she could possibly eat any herself, since the mouth in the huge plastic head was level with her eyes?

Ellie caught sight of her reflection in the glass office door and groaned. "I look an absolute . . . wally."

"Exactly!" Miss Cullins actually smiled.

Ellie picked up the basket of eggs and the umbrella and headed for the stairs, vowing to look at her job description as soon as this was over.

Once she was outside, though, her spirits lifted. It really was beautiful weather, and soon it would be Easter.

She headed for the entrance, where visitors were still streaming in. Then, looking round furtively, she hid the umbrella in the nearest bush. She simply couldn't make her glasses spin, hold a basket and give out eggs while also holding a brolly.

The park was full of excited children who were thrilled to see her (and her chocolate eggs), and Ellie had her photo taken over and over again.

"Thank you!" the children called happily.

"Bet you're hot under that lot, mate," their fathers said, grinning and assuming the person under the costume must be a man.

"They're not very big eggs," one boy said rudely from behind her, and Ellie turned, struggling to keep her face pleasant.

Then she remembered that her Wally face was smiling relentlessly, and so she allowed herself a private glare inside the costume.

"Hey! I remember you," she said. "You've already had one, so don't be greedy!"

The boy's hand shot out and he grabbed another egg from the basket and ran off.

"Boys will be boys," his mother said with a fond smile, and followed her son, who was throwing the brightly coloured foil wrapping on the ground.

As the day wore on, and Ellie replenished her basket countless times (keeping a careful eye out for the rude child, who seemed to be following her), she grew hotter and hotter.

At last, though, the park was emptying, and Ellie headed back to her office, desperate to take off the uncomfortable outfit. The huge wellies had nearly tripped her up several times, and her arms were aching from the heavy basket.

Suddenly, when she was nearly at the building that housed her dingy office, the rude boy ran out in front of her, tripping her up on purpose with the umbrella she'd hidden hours before.

She could feel her arms and legs flailing as if in slow motion, and saw the basket fly through the air as she tried not to collide with the child.

"You should look where you're going," his mother said angrily to her, and she led her son away without a backwards glance.

After that things happened fast.

An ambulance arrived (summoned by Miss Cullins, who had seen the whole thing through the window), and Ellie was bundled into it by a paramedic who, she noticed, despite being in pain, had the physique of a rugby player.

A rugby player with very kind brown eyes and a beautiful smile, and whose name, according to his badge, was Stephen.

"We'll soon have you comfortable, don't worry, mate," he said sympathetically. "Better have an X-ray just to check there's no lasting harm done. Can you take your head off for me?"

Ellie lifted her arm and squawked loudly, tears springing to her eyes. The man frowned.

"Please tell me there's not a girl under all this paraphernalia," he said, looking aghast.

He eased the plastic head off and removed the vast boots, then started to unpeel the layers of striped fur and cushions, looking more and more horrified.

"I think you've broken your arm. And possibly your wrist as well," he said, shaking his head. "It's amazing you didn't suffocate in there. It can't be legal."

Whether it was from shock or the effect of the painkillers he'd just given her, Ellie burst into tears.

"Oh, sweetheart, please don't cry," he said, stroking her hand very gently. "In a moment the painkillers will kick in, and we're nearly there."

And despite the pain which rocketed up her arm every time the ambulance hit a bump in the road, Ellie found herself wishing that he'd call her "sweetheart" again. When she wasn't dressed as Wally the Wabbit, maybe.

It turned out to be quite a complicated fracture – in addition to the expected broken wrist – and Ellie was kept in hospital overnight.

Her mother visited the following morning and was appalled.

"Your boss made you wear that ugly outfit all day? Is that legal?"

Ellie smiled weakly.

"That's what the paramedic said."

Her mother frowned.

"There was a paramedic in reception when I arrived. He was asking about a girl he'd picked up from the theme park yesterday, but he couldn't remember her surname, and the receptionist wasn't being very helpful.

"I thought he was talking about a child, but I suppose that might have been you, mightn't it?

"I thought it was a bit of a coincidence . . ."

"What?" Ellie squealed. "Mum! How many accidents do you think we get at the park in a day?

"Of course it was me! Where is he now?"

In her hospital gown and fluffy pink slippers, Ellie jumped out of bed, and ran out of the ward and down to the main entrance.

There were several paramedics standing by an ambulance, and Ellie headed towards them.

"Ellie!"

And there he was, with his wonderful smile that was imprinted on her memory, helped by the fact that she'd thought about him pretty solidly for the 17 hours since she'd last seen him – not that she was counting.

He was holding a bunch of pink tulips.

"I brought you these. But why aren't you in bed? Or at least sitting nice and still somewhere?" he asked, grinning at her.

He shepherded her back to her ward, handed the flowers to a nurse to put in a vase and politely answered her mother's rather probing questions.

Her mother was doing her best to ignore Ellie's pointed looks, but at last she left.

"It's really nice of you to come to check up on me, but don't you need to go as well?" Ellie said, trying not to sound as if she were desperate for him to stay. "Don't you have to work?"

"I've just come off duty," Stephen replied. "I was afraid you might already have been discharged. I wouldn't have known where to find you if you'd left."

"They're pretty hot on data protection here, so they wouldn't have given me your address.

"I would have had to hack into the hospital computer," Stephen teased mischievously, "and I'm not that good with IT, so I'm hoping you'll just tell me where you live so that I can see you again. Maybe in normal clothes?"

* * * *

And she had. Rather often, in fact.

She and Stephen spent every available moment together as spring morphed into early summer.

They went out for meals, walked in the park, watched old movies, had days at the seaside – it didn't matter what they did, as long as they were together.

Ellie was off work for almost two months, and when she went back to the theme park Miss Cullins was a changed woman.

It turned out that she had – with the office door firmly locked – tried on the Wally costume, and been appalled at what Ellie had endured.

She'd also realised – in Ellie's absence – what a lot of work she did.

"She's even asked me to call her Dorothy," Ellie told Stephen, laughing, when she'd been back a week. "She's not so bad, really."

Ellie had expected him to be less forgiving, but to her surprise he nodded.

"No, I'm sure you're right. I think we ought to invite her to our wedding."

That had been a year ago.

A year filled with joy and happiness greater than Ellie had imagined possible, and which had included a great many bunches of pink tulips as well as a rather more formal, and romantic, proposal.

And here she was, about to walk up the aisle on the arm of her father.

The organ struck up the wedding march.

The congregation turned to watch the bride's progress, and a lump rose in Ellie's throat as she saw so many smiling friends and relations.

He mother was looking proud, dabbing at her eyes under a large hat.

Just a couple of pews behind her, Miss Cullins, in an equally large hat, was looking every bit as proud.

Stephen had put her name at the very top of the guest list.

"Well, without her we would never have met, would we? We owe her a great deal."

Ellie looked beyond her boss to where Stephen was standing next to his best man, and her heart swelled.

"Sweetheart, you look . . . amazing," he whispered, smiling down at his beautiful bride. ∎

Vintage Cleaning Tips from the "Friend"

Salt

COMMON table salt, calcium chloride, does more than flavour your food; it's been an invaluable cleaning aid for centuries. Absorbent, abrasive and with disinfectant properties, it's a boon for anyone who wants to keep their home clean and green, as it's both natural and non-toxic. Our grannies and great-grannies knew a thing or two about eco-friendly home care!

Back in their day, open fires meant that your carpet was in constant danger of sooty stains. But never fear, the "Friend" advised in 1957, "Cover the affected part lightly with salt or dry starch. Leave for a short time then brush up with a clean brush."

Before we had ballpoint pens or notepad apps on our smartphones, the use of ink created a daily hazard for carpets and other textiles. Salt came to the rescue again in 1915. In the event of a spill, we said, "Throw a quantity of salt on it, which will quickly absorb the ink. Take this up and put on more salt. Keep repeating, rubbing salt well into the ink spot, until ink is all taken up by the salt. Then brush the salt out of the carpet."

Domestic disasters of the fatty kind could be averted with swift recourse to the salt container: "If you spill hot fat on a wooden surface, pour salt over it immediately," the "Friend" said in 1961. "The salt soaks up the fat and prevents it sinking into the wood and marking it."

Metals, too, benefited from an application of salt. How annoying to find rust on your flat irons in 1882. But they could be kept smooth and sparkling with a little beeswax and salt: "Tie a lump of wax in a rag and keep it for that purpose. When the irons are hot, rub them first with the wax rag, then scour with a paper or cloth sprinkled with salt."

Readers in 1966 were reassured to note that, "Badly neglected brass can be cleaned with a cut lemon dipped in salt. Rub hard with the lemon, then wash at once in hot, soapy water and polish."

Stains and spills – they've had their chips. ∎

Maypole Magic

by Barbara Dynes

W**HEN** I recently joined the PTA at my daughter's school, I must confess I thought of it as just another "activity" – yet one more to add to all the many extra things I'd determinedly packed into my life since Paul left us to be with Sarah.

My friend, Anne, had earnestly advised me that was definitely the way to go.

"Fill every minute, Claire," she said. "That's the answer to a broken heart."

I'm not so sure about that, I think now, studying the blank faces of other committee members around this table. But – luckily enough – I do quite enjoy being involved in school events, as it turns out.

Today, the PTA have got together to discuss the May Day fete, coming up soon. Mrs Jakes, the head teacher, has decided that the visitors to the school need to be impressed, and thus will need entertained.

I have a sudden brainwave.

"Maypole dancing!" I exclaim. "We did it at my old school. The children and parents loved it!"

Every head swivels my way. Almost every face looks puzzled, confused or downright unimpressed.

I stop, embarrassed.

That's ancient history, Claire, I remind myself – they won't want to know! But, to my surprise, everyone turns out to be keen and the idea is adopted.

* * * *

But I should have known there would be a hitch. One day, I'm just home from work when Mrs Jakes rings me.

"I'm sorry, but Asti, our maintenance man, isn't happy," she states.

"He's tried to make a maypole, but says he hasn't a clue how to string one together – the pole, ribbons, etcetera.

"The last thing I want to do is to upset him – he's such a good worker. I'm sure you understand. So sadly we might have to abandon your great idea."

I sympathise for a bit, then ring off and make myself a coffee.

My Paul – correction, my ex, Paul – could have saved the day. By helping Asti, I mean.

"He can turn his hand to anything, your Paul," Mum used to say in admiration.

My own father hadn't been much use around the house.

"Well, Mum, he's now 'turning his hand' to a new relationship and living miles away," I mutter aloud, taking a second biscuit as consolation.

OK, I know Paul would probably still help, if asked, but there's no way I'm getting him involved.

* * * *

When I tell my daughter that the maypole dancing is doomed, Olivia is devastated. She was so looking forward to wearing her new swirly lime green skirt.

"We could suggest that Asti looks for instructions online," I say, clutching at straws.

My old-fashioned ten-year-old pooh-poohs that idea.

"What about my 'Pastimes' book, the one you put in the attic?" she declares. "It had all about May Day and dancing in there. Sticking a

A Weather Forecaster

The weather is putting
My plans into doubt –
It started to rain
But now the sun's out.

I'm wanting a walk,
But what outfit will do?
It's hot, then it's cold;
Sky's dark, now it's blue.

Decisions, decisions;
Nothing's simple or plain,
And all for the sake
Of a walk down the lane.

I'll take an umbrella
As a compromise to
Whatever the weather's
Intending to do.

My life's been so busy
Since I chose to retire,
Spent mostly deciding
What clothes I require.

John Darley

maypole together and all that!"

Out comes the ladder and down comes the dusty book.

And, yes, joy of joys, there are somewhat detailed diagrams – though it's a bit more complicated than just "sticking a maypole together", as you might expect.

But Olivia thinks she's solved the problem and, one day after school, we take the book to Asti's workshop.

"Asti!" I yell through the open door.

Funny name, Asti. It's short for Sebastian, a teacher once told me. The man himself – the tall, fair, silent type – suddenly appears, frowning at us through a musky haze of wood shavings and dust.

"Hi! I've come about the maypole. We thought Olivia's book might help. I feel responsible, seeing as it was my idea in the first place," I finish lamely.

Olivia eagerly hands over "Pastimes", which Asti accepts slowly and with a deep sense of suspicion. Then I show him a black-and-white photo.

"That's my late gran as a girl in the 1940s, dancing on May Day," I say, pointing. "A good close-up of a maypole, eh?"

Asti just stares, and I panic. Who do I think I am, telling this man how to do his job?

Then, grunting something inaudible, he nods at us to come inside.

Wow, what a chaotic Aladdin's cave of a workshop we are stepping into! Shelves of paint tins and tools, planks of wood . . . and a table piled high with brightly coloured ribbons – scarlet, blue, green, yellow – like so many flags of so many nations.

"I hope I get a red one." Olivia breaks off, staring at the floor, strewn with broken bits of artificial flowers and wire. "Oh, you've dropped the flowers!"

"Threw them, more like." Asti shrugs and then grins. "I tried copying a posy for the top of the pole from an online picture. Disaster!"

"Books are best," Olivia says wisely.

"You do have a maypole, though, Asti," I remark brightly, nodding towards the innards from a roll of carpet propped against the wall.

"Well, yes – I suppose it's a start," he admits grudgingly. "But you try fixing those ribbons to this 'crown'!"

Despairingly, he indicates notches he's made on a separate wooden attachment.

"And you're supposed to put flowers on top." He shakes his head. "Give me electrical stuff or a leaking pipe to mend any day."

He peers again at my photo.

"I must say, those kiddies do look as though they're loving the dancing."

I seize my chance.

"Yes, Olivia was so looking forward to it." I risk a glance at his face.

Strike while the iron's hot, Claire, I tell myself, indicating another little girl in the picture.

"That's my gran's friend, Liz Burkett. She told me stories about many a happy May Day in the past.

"Liz is in her eighties and lived in the village, but we lost touch when she moved."

"Oh!" Asti suddenly smiles and I blink in surprise. It's an unexpectedly warm, friendly smile.

"What a small world! I used to do Mrs Burkett's garden," he goes on. "She's a really lovely lady. She moved to Blue Skies Home in Drayton."

"Did she really?" I exclaim in delight. "Oh, I must go and see her again."

Asti continues to study the book for a few minutes. Then he nods slowly.

"Oh, OK then – I'll tell Mrs Jakes I'll have another go. Just for you, Olivia."

He winks at her and she beams.

As we leave, Asti thanks Olivia for the loan of the book. Then he grins at me, lifting one eyebrow really comically.

I find myself blushing as I return the grin.

* * * *

Back home, I can't seem to get May Day out of my head. Which, I realise ruefully, is a welcome change from nagging thoughts of Paul and his new girlfriend, Sarah.

And I've had another idea. But one that will only pay off if Asti manages to construct the maypole . . .

When Olivia comes home chatting about plaiting ribbons and practising her dancing, I put my plan into action.

After school on the Thursday before Saturday's fete, Olivia and I go to the woods to pick some wildflowers.

Later, she helps me weave florist's wire amongst large yellow daisies, bluebells, grasses and ferns.

The resulting posy, though colourful enough, and I suppose quite pretty, still seems amateurish to me, but Olivia declares it "amazing", which gives me courage.

* * * *

Next day, though, Asti is not in his workshop. He'll be setting up the maypole on the school playing field, I tell myself.

Let's hope he's managed to finish it without too much bother or he'll be blaming me.

I lay my flowers outside, and pin on a note: *Made this, if it's any use? Claire.*

* * * *

Saturday is sunny and warm. Paul, who intended coming to see Olivia dance, has had to cry off through work.

Olivia is disappointed, of course, but I, for once, feel OK about him not being here, Maybe I'm getting used to the situation at last, I think, feeling a little flicker of hope.

Leaving Olivia – in her green skirt and scarlet top – with her pals, I mingle with the crowd.

Mrs Jakes greets me.

"The children are so excited!" She laughs. "There's no sign of Asti at the moment, but the maypole looks fantastic.

"This was a great idea, Claire, thank you!"

I gaze beyond the various stalls to the makeshift stage and my heart misses a beat . . . because my home-made crown is sitting majestically on top of the pole!

In all its gold, blue and green glory, it looks great.

But where is Asti?

As I watch Mrs Jakes opening the fete, something occurs to me, and I frown.

Just musing on the odd name, Asti, seems to do something weird to my insides. Something quite deliciously weird . . .

*   *   *   *

Much later, the dancing is about to start when I feel a tap on my shoulder.

"Claire, I've brought someone to see you."

As I turn, three things register.

Asti's blue T-shirt is a perfect match for his eyes, my stomach is somersaulting like crazy . . . and beside him is a face I haven't seen in a very long time.

"Claire! Lovely to see you again!" Liz cries.

Delighted, I thank Asti and hug Liz, noting her careful make-up and still-wonderful skin.

Then the music strikes up and the stage is a sudden kaleidoscope of colour as the children begin to dance.

Liz is soon wiping away tears and I feel a bit choked myself at the happy scene.

"Your little Olivia . . . she could be me!" she cries. "Oh, it's wonderful to see the young ones keeping up the maypole tradition – takes me right back!"

I'm busy taking pictures so that Liz can have lasting memories when Asti touches my hand.

"I'd like to thank you for that lovely posy, and Olivia for loaning me her book," he says gruffly.

He hesitates.

"Do you think maybe I could take you both out somewhere nice, one day soon?"

I don't need to think about it.

"That would be lovely," I say at once, and beam at Asti. And this time, I notice happily, he's the one who is blushing.

As the children finish their dancing, a great cheer goes up from the crowd.

And me? For some reason, I feel as though I've just been crowned May Queen . . . ∎

Shutterstock.

Making Music

by Pamela Ormondroyd

I 'M sure you'd really enjoy it, love."

Katie Henderson smiled sweetly at her gran but remained tight-lipped.

"I mean, you do have a lovely voice, darling," Diana continued, "and this new singing class could be just the ticket to buck you up. It says on the leaflet that singing is a real feel-good tonic. Won't you at least give it a try?"

Katie sighed.

"Oh, Gran, I know you're just trying to help but I don't even feel like talking to anyone just now, let alone singing with them!"

"Katie, love." Diana sat down next to her sad-looking granddaughter and took her hand. "I know you've had a tough time recently, with all the redundancy talk at work and then with that selfish rogue Martin going off with that horrid –"

"Yes, all right, Gran. Please don't remind me. Anyway, I'm not upset that much any more, just angry with myself for being such a fool."

"Well, staying at home and nursing that anger isn't good for you. It's not healthy. You need to get back out there, show your pretty face, meet friends, have fun.

"Look, if it helps at all, I'll come along to the first singing session with you. Moral support and all that."

"Chaperone, you mean?" Katie said, managing a faint smile. "In case I'm silly enough to be attracted to any more rogues?"

"Not at all," Diana said, clearing the cups away. "It's because I love you, that's all, and hate to see you unhappy." She picked up the tray and took it out into the kitchen, where she stopped for a moment in the doorway.

"Though I must say I'm quite intrigued myself. I used to enjoy a bit of am-dram in my time; a little dancing and singing with the chorus. So, will you at least think about it, Katie?"

Katie sighed deeply.

"All right, I'll think about it," she said.

Diana entered the kitchen with a smile on her face. There was a glimmer of hope. The battle was almost won.

* * * *

"Oh, for goodness' sake, Brian. I'll be the oldest there."

"Nonsense. There's no age limit on singing, Pops. The leaflet says everyone is welcome."

"My voice isn't up to it any more. It's too thin. I can't hit the notes."

"That's only because you haven't used it properly for yonks."

"Nothing like it was when I was in the police choir," Gerald said, looking quite deflated. "Rich and melodic it was then. I used to sing solos."

"And you could again, Pops. And wouldn't Gran be proud to hear you exercising those vocal cords once more? She'd be all for you getting out and enjoying yourself. You couldn't keep her in, remember?"

Gerald nodded and his eyes lit up. Grace had always been the driving force, getting them into ballroom dancing, bowls, book and theatre groups.

But now she wasn't around any more to give him a gentle shove, Gerald's confidence had taken a knock and he'd become a little reclusive.

"And you won't have to talk to anyone there because you'll all be singing, won't you?" Brian persevered.

Gerald went quiet for a moment.

"No, I can't go anyway, Brian. Can't even get there. The bus doesn't go past the library any more."

"No problem, I'll run you there. It's my half day and I've nothing else planned."

Gerald eyed his persistent grandson as the boy studied the music leaflet. He was a good, kind-hearted lad but had inherited the full-blown stubbornness of his beloved gran.

There was no use arguing. Brian seemed to have every angle covered. Well, he'd give the class a go just this once. And once only!

* * * *

Marion Ashworth was a little nervous. It was always a bit of a gamble getting a new class up and running. You never knew if anyone had bothered to read the posters or picked up a leaflet or had even decided to turn up!

The library had been most helpful, letting her use the little side room free of charge for the first session or two to see how it went, but Marion knew that if the group wasn't viable after that it would be a non-starter.

She took a deep breath, put out the chairs and placed a few sheets of music on each. She had chosen a varied, easy programme for starters, an ensemble of popular songs that most folk would know.

Somewhere in the middle of the session, they would have a short break to get to know each other. If anyone came, that was!

Marion picked up her guitar and tuned it and then checked her tablet for backing tracks. The clock ticked on. Fifteen minutes to go.

The door opened just a little and a young man's head appeared.

"Oh, I'm sorry," he said. "We seem to be a bit early." He looked about and appeared surprised at the empty room. "Have we got the right room? Is this the choir session?"

Marion smiled and nodded.

"Oh, do come in," she said. "I'm Marion, your leader for the session. So pleased to see you. Please take a seat."

"Actually, I'm not the one staying," Brian said, as Gerald held back, almost hidden behind his grandson. "I've just brought my grandad and then I'm off."

"That's a shame," Marion said. "I do like a mixed class. It makes it so much more interesting and we do learn such a lot from each other."

"Well, you could stay just this once, Brian, couldn't you?" Gerald said, suddenly deciding to become visible. "I mean, you did say you'd got nothing else planned."

Brian blushed and stared at his grandad.

"Well, then, that's settled." Marion smiled. "Take a pew, both of you." And before he knew it, Brian was seated next to Pops in the front row.

"Don't be shy, Brian," she added. "I don't bite!"

Two ladies entered the room next and introduced themselves, and they had only just settled down behind Gerald and Brian when two more couples walked into the room.

Marion's heart lifted. She already had eight singers and there was still a little time to go. Not bad at all for a first session!

From experience she knew that many choirs grew mainly on the strength of recommendation, and if the folk here today enjoyed themselves as much as she hoped, news would spread and her numbers would gradually increase.

She picked up her guitar and began to strum and the gentle chatter subsided.

Suddenly, the door opened once more and a small lady with a friendly face entered, followed by a rather sullen-looking young woman.

"So sorry we're late," the smiling face said. "We couldn't find a parking place. I'm Diana, and my granddaughter is called Katie."

"No problem." Marion smiled. "I'm pleased to see you both. Come down here in the front."

Diana walked confidently to the front of the room and plonked herself down next to Gerald, offering her hand whilst, head low, Katie dawdled behind and perched nervously on the end seat, as if she was liable to take flight at any moment.

"Well, I must say it's lovely to see you all here today, so thank you so much for making the effort." Marian addressed her class.

"Now, I realise that some of you may not have done much singing for a while, so this first lesson is really just to get those tonsils lubricated once again.

"You will have found a list of around ten songs on your sheets which I hope you will already be acquainted with, so please don't be shy. Sing your hearts out, add any harmonies if you wish, but let's just have a good old singsong today and then take it from there.

"This group is not about perfection, it's all about having fun and feeling good."

∗   ∗   ∗   ∗

It was obvious after the first few numbers that Gerald and Diana were enjoying themselves a lot more than their grandchildren.

Gerald was in fine voice, suddenly rediscovering his vocal range and giving a powerful edge to the proceedings.

Diana looked across appreciatively and he smiled back, and they joined up together in perfect harmony for the final number before a short coffee break.

Indeed, after the song had ended it was greeted with enthusiastic applause from the other singers and Marion was completely overwhelmed.

"Well, it looks like we've got ourselves a couple of professionals, folks." She chuckled. "So, you two, Diana and Gerald, must definitely come again!" They both beamed.

As the group dispersed for a break, Brian caught Katie's eye across the row. Katie pulled a bit of a face and Brian smiled, and then Katie pointed her head in the direction of the refreshment table.

Brian responded and both youngsters got up together and made for the tea urn in the corner.

"Well, at least your grandma and Pops seem to be enjoying themselves," Brian remarked a little nervously.

Katie looked across at Diana and Gerald and her face broke into a smile.

"So it wasn't an entirely wasted morning after all." She grinned.

The young man beside her seemed as uncomfortable as she was. She suddenly noticed he seemed quite nice and did have rather a lovely, cheerful face.

"My grandmother dragged me here, thinking it would do me good," she said.

"I've been a bit low recently what with work worries and other things. I must say they all seem friendly enough, but this is definitely not my scene."

"Nor mine," Brian agreed, thinking what a nice girl she was. "Old Pops has been quite down, too, since he lost my gran. And I know he used to enjoy a good old singsong."

Brian paused for a moment.

"Look, if you're not bothered about staying for the second half, there's a nice little coffee shop next door. How about we pop out for half an hour?"

"Sounds good to me." Katie took one last look at her grandma and saw how she was happily engaged in conversation with Gerald and Marion.

"I don't think they'll miss us at all!"

* * * *

Marion was very happy after the first session. Everyone seemed to enjoy themselves and all promised to spread the word and return the following week.

She was especially impressed with Gerald and Diana, thinking how they would prove to be a big asset to the group and wondering if she might soon be able to get some lovely harmonies going.

She wasn't too sure about the youngsters, though. She'd noticed them slip out at break and then return rather sheepishly later to pick up their grandparents.

But she was quietly amused, thinking that it might not be too long before that pair were making sweet music of their own! That was the magic of song. It worked its spell in all manner of ways.

* * * *

"So, will you be going back to choir next week, Gran?" Katie asked later that evening.

"Oh, you just try to stop me, darling." Diana grinned. "They are a lovely crowd, especially that sweet Gerald, and he's saving me a seat for next time. Though I'm sorry it didn't quite work out for you, Katie."

"Oh, I don't know about that." Katie smiled to herself. She was already looking forward to meeting up with Brian in the coffee bar again very soon.

"I rather enjoyed myself. It was a great idea, that singing class, Gran. I'm feeling tons better already!" ■

Bristol

Bristol is steeped in history. From Pero's Bridge, named to honour enslaved African Pero Jones, to the first female doctor, Elizabeth Blackwell, you'll find much to admire about this waterside city.

Isambard Kingdom Brunel was involved in the design of the Clifton Suspension Bridge spanning the Avon Gorge – he was aged just twenty-four when he took on this massive project. The suspension bridge was also the location of Britain's first bungee jump!

Bristol also has a fascinating maritime history, not least of all the fact it's home to *SS Great Britain* – a revolutionary steamship designed by Brunel whose transatlantic route took passengers from Bristol to New York City. Going further back in time, the famous pirate Blackbeard is also thought to have been born here in 1680.

A tour of Bristol's many museums will uncover so much more about this fascinating city, which was also the birthplace of Hollywood actor Cary Grant – whose real name was the less glamorous-sounding Archibald Leach!

Come And Join Us

by Donald Lightwood

T HE first sight spectators got of the march from the crowded pavement was of hats, most of them large, round and straw. The marchers were Suffragettes, demanding votes for women as they processed down Knightsbridge.

Three girls were in the watching crowd: Vi, a barmaid, Lucy, a laundress, and Edie, a flower seller when she was lucky. All three, aged seventeen and eighteen, were in their Sunday best, and none of them was particularly interested in the marchers and their posh ways.

Set in 1914

"I'm watch-out today," Vi said. "Got your bags?"

They nodded, and together they made their way behind the crowd on the pavement.

The most noticeable feature of the marching women was their clothes. Their tailored suits and dresses spoke more of the fashion trends of 1914 than of protest. However, their banners and slogans proclaimed their cause.

"It should be all right now," Vi said, and the girls slipped into one of the new department stores.

They went upstairs to the ladies' department and found that the customers and staff were crowded at the windows overlooking the street, watching the march.

This suited the girls perfectly. It wasn't the first time they'd used a Suffragette rally as a distraction to allow them to do a little shoplifting.

Vi pretended to be looking out of the window while the other two made their way around the counters, taking what they fancied. Then Vi noticed one of the women leave the march and come towards the store.

She moved to fetch the girls; it was time to get away. They headed for the stairs, but at the top they were halted by the woman Vi had spotted.

Illustration by Mandy Dixon.

She was expensively dressed in white, with a hat decorated with feathers, kept in place by a fine net scarf. Round her chest she had a sash with *National Society For Women's Suffrage* printed on it.

"I would like to see what you have got in the bag you are trying to hide under your coat," she said to Lucy.

"I ain't got nothing and it ain't none of your business, anyway," Lucy told her.

"It's very much my business, since my name is Roberta Billington and my family owns this department store."

The girls exchanged glances with each other.

"You, too," the woman added to Edie.

"They didn't mean to do nothing bad," Vi said.

"Then they won't mind emptying their bags."

Roberta Billington had the girls at her mercy. They might have had on their best clothes, but they didn't fool her. They were obviously up from the East End.

Recognising defeat, Lucy and Edie gave up their bags. They stood with lowered heads, avoiding Roberta's gaze.

"You realise I could have you prosecuted for what you have done?" she told them.

"We're sorry," Vi said.

"No, you're not. Please don't waste time lying. Have you done this sort of thing before?" Roberta asked.

Vi nodded.

"That's better. Now you are being honest. Let's keep it that way."

"What's going to happen to us?" Edie blurted out.

Roberta was well aware of their fear. The law was hard – too hard, in her opinion, on the poorer classes. She pointed at her sash.

"Do you know what this means?" she asked.

"You want women to able to vote," Lucy said.

"Correct. In addition to that, we want to improve conditions for women. Get rid of discrimination."

"It don't make no difference to the likes of us," Vi muttered.

Roberta let out a sigh.

"And that is the problem in a nutshell." She clasped her hands together. "It was inevitable that the movement would be created by articulate, middle-class women, but in spite of appearances, we are concerned for all women."

The girls stood awkwardly in front of her, still wondering about their fate.

Vi screwed up her courage.

"Are you going to tell the coppers?"

Roberta had momentarily forgotten why they were there. She shook her head.

"I would like to think you were putting your energy into something more worthwhile. I appreciate that life may be difficult for you. But even so . . ."

"You mean you ain't going to turn us in?" Edie said, incredulous.

Roberta nodded, and then smiled at the relief on their faces. She noted that they didn't say thank you.

"Can we go, then?" Vi asked.

"Yes, but promise to think about what I have told you."

"What do you mean?"

"About the women's movement," Roberta said. "You are exactly the young women we need to reach. We need to show people we care for everybody."

The girls lingered in the crowd outside the store. The march had halted and degenerated into a seething mass. The Suffragette ranks had been invaded and the police were trying to break up scuffling groups.

"Blimey, look at that!" Vi cried. A man was attacking a woman with the pole from her banner.

"Leave her alone, you rotten pig!" Edie yelled at him.

Another woman pushed her way through the crush to help.

"It's her!" Vi shouted. "Look, it's her!"

Roberta Billington was tall for a woman and it helped her to take on the man. She grabbed the pole and pushed with all her strength. Taken by surprise, the man lost his balance and fell down.

Roberta ended their struggle by cracking him on the shins with the pole.

Shutterstock.

Sun's Rays

We're going to the seaside
On this lovely summer's day,
The treasure there just waiting
To shoo our cares away.
The gentle rolling of the tide
The rhythmic ebb and flow,
The sea a brighter olive shade
With hint of rosy glow.
The seaweed scent is wonderful,
Our senses start to swim,
We feel its healing balm,
The good in everything.
A tasty crab, a pretty shell
By the rock pools shining green,
Time stands still, magic flows,
We're in the seaside dream.
The sweeping gulls spot their lunch,
The fresh fish they adore,
Big catches in the trawler boats
From the mighty ocean floor.
And on the shimmering shoreline
And foaming filigree,
A paddle, with our loved ones,
And we touch eternity.

Dorothy McGregor

Vi, Lucy and Edie led the cheers. But then, to their dismay, they saw a group of policemen heading for Roberta.

* * * *

The girls took time off from work so that they could go to the police court. Along with several other women, Roberta had been charged with creating an affray in Knightsbridge.

A clever solicitor spoke in her defence, but an equally clever one led the prosecution. When he accused Roberta of having committed an attack on a defenceless man, the girls went wild.

They stood up in the public gallery and shouted to the magistrate that the man was lying. They were bundled into a corridor.

"Get your hands off me!" Vi shrieked at the court official.

"I could have you nicked for contempt of court!" he shouted back.

"No, you couldn't," a cool female voice said. "Leave them alone, or I shall have you charged for assaulting them."

The struggle ceased and a well-dressed young woman led them outside.

"That's better," she said. "I'm Maud Carmichael. Thank you for what you did in there. Roberta would have been grateful."

"He was lying!" Edie said.

"It's a male habit when it concerns our movement," Maud replied ruefully. "Let me treat you to a cup of tea."

The girls followed her into an elegant tea room they would never normally have dreamed of entering.

"So you support our cause?" Maud asked, once they were seated.

"We seen what happened to Miss Billington," Vi told her.

"She was dead brave," Lucy put in.

"She went at him like a bloke," Edie agreed. "You see women have a go down the pub sometimes. But not often."

"The problem is that basically we are against violence – particularly against women, of course," Maud told them, pouring tea.

"He asked for it!"

"I'm sure," Maud said. "We try to be peaceful, but sometimes circumstances are against us."

"Miss, can I have one of them cakes?" Edie asked.

"Of course. That's what they're there for."

Each of the girls took a cake.

"Where are you from?"

"Bethnal Green."

"We're hoping to start a group in East London," Maud went on. "Would you be interested in joining?"

They stopped chewing.

"It won't do no good," Vi said eventually. "It ain't for us. Not really."

"Of course it is!" Maud responded. "You're women."

Vi shook her head.

"You're posh – educated. We're like chalk and cheese, you lot and us."

To her surprise, Maud smiled.

"So why did you support Roberta in the court?"

"She was good to us," Lucy said.

"I think blokes like that should be sorted out," Edie added.

Maud nodded.

"And isn't that two very good reasons for joining us?"

Vi saw that Maud had spread her napkin on her lap. She'd been wondering what you did with it.

"It'd be like joining the bosses," she said.

Maud offered them more of the dainty little cakes.

"You know that Roberta will almost certainly be sent to prison?" The girls didn't respond. "She's already done time in Holloway.

"She's determined nothing will stop us," Maud added. "She's a dedicated woman."

"It said in the paper they go on hunger strike," Edie said, after a pause.

"Yes, and they are force fed," Maud told her. "It's as good as torture. People don't realise what they suffer."

"It shouldn't be allowed!" Vi exclaimed hotly.

Maud sat back in her chair.

"Exactly."

There was yet another silence from the girls.

"Look, I know there's a gulf between us," Maud said earnestly. "But could you at least spread the word? Tell people what you have seen. The injustice, about Roberta. In the pubs, at work, wherever."

The girls looked at each other.

"Yeah, all right," Vi said. "Thanks for the tea. We got to get back now."

* * * *

To Vi, Holloway Prison looked like a castle from the olden days that she remembered from pictures at school. She couldn't imagine how anybody could escape. It made you shiver to look at it.

The wide street outside the prison was filling up with women, there to protest about Roberta Billington's six-month sentence. Vi had argued with her friends about joining the protest, but they had backed off.

So she had come by herself, drawn by the knowledge that but for Roberta, they might have been the ones in prison.

Unsure what to do, Vi simply stood on the street and let the crowd grow round her. The single-minded mood of the women bound them together, generating a feeling of strength.

There was a movement towards the prison gates, which led to a courtyard and the main entrance. A line of policemen guarded the gates and confronted the women, now giving voice to their anger.

Squashed in the crowd, Vi felt herself charged with purpose. How could the authorities not be impressed by such a demonstration?

"Hello! It's Vi, isn't it?" a posh voice cried out.

Maud Carmichael had suddenly appeared at Vi's side.

"It's good to see you," she said with a smile.

"It's a smashing crowd," Vi called back.

"Yes, let's hope the government takes note."

More women continued to join the throng. Unusually, there were no hostile spectators. Everybody present was there for the same reason – the unfair treatment of women.

Vi and Maud stayed together as the noise grew louder and throats grew sore. Surprisingly, a man appeared in front of the prison gates.

He was a magistrate and he began reading from a sheet of paper. Few could hear what he was saying.

"He's reading the Riot Act," Maud told Vi.

"What's that mean?" she said.

"Basically that they can arrest anybody they like if we don't clear off," Maud told her. "Stay with me and be ready to run."

Some mounted police joined their colleagues and set about breaking up the crowd. They had their truncheons drawn, threatening the women if they didn't move away from the prison.

Pandemonium broke out and the shouts for women's rights became terrified screams. There could be no fighting back. Escape was the only option.

One policeman had just been kicked and was swinging his baton around like a madman. He eyed Vi, but just as he was about to strike, Maud grabbed his arm and the blow glanced off Vi's shoulder.

Mercifully they were able to struggle to the edge of the crowd and run until they were gasping for breath and had to stop.

They were outside a pub. Without a word they staggered in, not caring what the customers thought. They flopped down on a free bench.

"What can I get you, ladies?" the landlord asked.

"What do they serve, in a place like this?" Maud asked Vi weakly.

Vi was rubbing her shoulder and wincing.

"Two halves of stout," she told the landlord.

"How's your shoulder?" Maud asked.

"I'll live," Vi said. "Thanks to you. He was going to hit me on the head."

They adjusted their hats and clothes. Hot and sweaty, they were glad to get their breathing back to normal.

"I hope today's experience hasn't put you off for ever," Maud said.

Vi shook her head.

"Not a bit. It's made my mind up – seeing women treated like that. It's wrong, the government allowing that."

Maud took Vi's hand.

"That's the spirit. You're one of us." She raised her glass. "Here's to victory!"

＊　＊　＊　＊

Not a lot happens on Sunday afternoons in Bethnal Green. And so it was a notable event when a boisterous march came snaking its way through the borough. Lucy and Edie watched it from a corner.

There was a large banner in the centre of the marchers saying who they were: *The East London Federation Of Suffragettes*. It was being carried by Vi and Maud.

"What are you doing there, Vi?" Edie shouted.

"What's it look like?" Vi retorted. "Votes For Women!"

"You ain't one of them now, are you?" Lucy shouted.

"She's helping the fight for justice," Maud responded. "You should be doing the same."

The women were relieved to hear more cheers than jeers as they marched along. The East End was unknown territory and they were hoping the Them and Us gap could be crossed.

From today's response it looked as if it might be.

"Come And Join Us," the marchers sang and many a working woman was doing just that.

"She's our mate," Lucy and Edie said, proudly pointing out Vi to the women beside them in the march's growing ranks.

"You on their side?" somebody asked.

"Not half!" Lucy replied. ■

Vintage Cleaning Tips from the "Friend"

Vinegar

VINEGAR seems to have more cleaning comebacks than most eco ingredients. A quick search on the website of a well-known book retailer reveals more than 200 currently available titles devoted to its use as a household cleaner. But "Friend" readers have been wise to the disinfecting, deodorising and grime-removing properties of this mild acid for over a century.

However, readers in 1915 who adopted a well-known tip to remove marking ink stains from cotton with a mixture of "chloride of lime and vinegar" would have been lucky to have escaped unscathed. Chloride of lime is a bleaching powder – sodium hypochlorite – and mixing vinegar, or any acid, with a chlorine-based bleach can release potentially lethal chlorine gas. Old-fashioned remedies can be bad for your health!

Much more successful was the 1921 recipe for furniture polish: "Equal parts of linseed oil, turpentine, vinegar and methylated spirits. Shake well. Ordinary salad oil and vinegar in equal parts also produces a very good polish."

You could overdo the polishing, though. In 1966, owners of older furniture that had become encrusted with dirt and old polish could remove those layers with a spring cleaning tip. "Wash out a cloth in a solution of vinegar and water, using one tablespoonful of vinegar to a quart of warm water. Wash the article of furniture and dry well. Smooth wax polish on evenly, being careful not to use too much. Leave it to dry slightly for a few minutes, then rub up with a soft cloth."

Vinegar was great for cleaning and deodorising glassware, too. Once you'd finished sprucing up your furniture in 1966, it was time to turn to your vases. "A large spoonful of salt in a little vinegar will clean glass vases coated inside and smelling of dead leaves. Shake the vase and leave for a few hours then rinse in clean water." Sparkling! ■

Older And Wiser

by Gabrielle Mullarkey

YCLES," my dad always says when we're stacking shelves together. "It's all about cycles, Kev."

Dad runs the village minimart and has lots of retail wisdom to impart. "Cycles" refers to phases that people go through, usually after a TV chef has popularised a certain kind of food or dish.

"Never stockpile canned exotica," Dad told me once, marking down unsold tinned wild anchovies.

"You live and learn, Kev, live and learn."

It's just me and Dad, so we're together a lot. Mum died when I was little, which was sad, but to be honest I barely remember her.

I have photos, so I know she was pretty, but I try not to think too much about her.

Everyone in the village (and Dad, I think) assumes that I'll take over the minimart one day; that he's training me up for it.

He took over running the shop from his dad back in the day, and if I pick up the baton (or pricing gun), he won't even have to change the Stevens & Son sign across our striped awning.

Grandad's up in the Oaks now, a care home a few miles away; Dad visits him twice a week and I go with him every other weekend.

I like to see him and I do like to hear his stories about what the shop was like when he was starting out.

But as I've got older, I've realised that I'll never want to run the minimart. I like the customers, but I can't see myself being tied to a career in retail, the way Dad is.

I've tried to drop hints.

"Did you ever want to be anything else, Dad?" I asked once.

"Oh, aye, I wanted to be all sorts," he acknowledged, sticking a pencil behind his ear. "Fan dancer, trapeze artist, international man of mystery."

Illustration by Helen Welsh.

I rolled my eyes.

"If you're not going to be serious . . ."

"Wildlife photographer," he amended, moving his sliding ladder along the stockroom shelves.

"That was my longest phase. Even applied to do a photography course at college once."

"I didn't know that! What happened?"

"Life." He laughed dolefully. "Your grandad's knees went, so he couldn't get up and down this ladder. I took over full-time and put college on the back burner."

He shrugged.

"Don't you feel you missed out, though?" I asked. This was a whole year ago, when I was thirteen and less sensitive to people's feelings.

"I mean, running a shop's a bit different from photographing tigers and giraffes, isn't it?"

"Maybe." Another shrug. "But then, one day, this knockout girl comes into the shop and asks for a quarter pound of pear drops and the rest, as they say, is history."

I love hearing how my parents met. Mum was only in the village visiting her aunt who, it turned out, was the one who liked pear drops.

But after meeting her future husband, my future mum kept finding reasons to bike over to our village from her dad's farm miles away. Her parents must have thought she was very fond of her aunt.

"What did Grandad say about you not going to college?" I asked.

"I told him there'd always be next year." Dad reached for his pencil.

"Mañana, mañana, Kev. Slipperiest word in the English language."

I was half-tempted to tell him it wasn't an English word, but I was too busy mulling over everything he'd said.

*   *   *   *

So anyway, it's a whole year later and I've a fair few things to worry about. Most of these worries sort of condense into one big ball of worry. School.

The good news is that I'm handy at most subjects; the bad news is that swotty kids aren't cool or popular.

There's this one girl in my class, Elinor Jenkins, who's totally lush. And I overheard a bunch of kids talking during one break about a big party she's having that "everyone" is invited to.

I tried not to earwig too closely for fear of looking like a sad case, but I did more intel gathering and learned that Elinor's parents have hired out practically a whole restaurant for her fourteenth birthday.

What's more, it's a restaurant in Stanhope, the biggest town round about, which is about 20 minutes away by train.

At this restaurant, apparently, everyone gets a chance to make their own pizza and there's a prize for the person who invents the best new topping.

I can't decide if that sounds lame or fun.

A few days later, I watch invites being handed out in class at the break.

I try not to count, but it does look as if everyone in the class is getting one (why didn't she just do the invites on social media, so it would be less obvious who she was leaving out?)

I feel pretty low for the rest of the day – even though logic tells me that obviously not everyone did get an invite. It just feels as if I'm the only one left out.

Then, on the bus home, Gary Hedgeley pounces. He's in my form class and he's two months younger than me, but he's quite a bit bigger and taller.

I usually manage to steer clear of him, but this day, as if I wasn't feeling bad enough, he gets me in a headlock, eventually lets me go and orders me to do his maths homework for the foreseeable future.

As this is preferable to the headlock, I agree.

I'm to start by giving him the answers to tonight's homework on the bus tomorrow morning, so he can copy them into his exercise book in his own hand.

I'd still rather be me than Gary Hedgeley, who will never know for himself where "y" is on the axis.

As I'm getting off the bus, thankfully leaving Gary to continue his journey, I hear a voice behind me.

I turn warily, and it's Beth Jones.

She lives in the village, not far from me, and we have history – sort of. Beth Jones is the first (and so far, only) girl I've kissed.

∗ ∗ ∗ ∗

I was star-gazing one night last summer in the village park, when she came up on her bike.

"What you doing there, Kevin Stevens?"

I wasn't intimidated because she's often been in our shop, sometimes with her mum.

So I showed her Venus through the telescope that Dad got me last Christmas, and that must have impressed her, because she leant over her handlebars and kissed me.

Just like that and without any warning.

∗ ∗ ∗ ∗

Now, as soon as I turn at the bus drop-off, Beth clocks me.

"What happened to your braces?"

"They came off for good last month," I tell her.

Beth hasn't seen me for a while. She goes to an all-girls' school in the opposite direction to mine.

"Cool." She nods. "So, Kev, are you going to this Jenkins shindig on Friday night, up in Stanhope?"

"I might." I shrug, as if I've had loads of competing better offers.

"How do you know Elinor?" I ask curiously. "You're at different schools."

"Oh, our mums sing in the same choir," Beth replies airily. "I hope you will come, Kev."

Something (either honesty or a self-destructive streak) makes me confess.

"I haven't had an invite."

Some of my peers would have recoiled then, as if my unpopularity was contagious. But not Beth.

"Never mind about that, it's word of mouth, I was told. Elly said her whole form class is invited. Aren't you in her form class?"

I can't fault her logic, but then, Beth has cheek and confidence and all the other qualities I can't seem to develop.

She walks with me as far as the fork in the road that leads to her big posh house, the Willows.

"Who's that boy I saw you talking to on the bus?" she asks casually.

I cast my mind back.

"Gary Hedgeley?" I shudder. "He was doing all the talking."

"Is he in your class?"

I admit that he is, and to my dismay, Beth gets a faraway, dreamy look in her eyes.

Why, I wonder, do lads like Gary hold such an allure for otherwise rational and intelligent females?

Now that I've run into Beth, though, I am considering her advice to just turn up at the restaurant on Friday night. It's not really my style, but maybe it should be?

Back home, I stand in front of my bedroom mirror and practise various scenarios involving me breezing up to Elinor in the restaurant, handing her a rope-handled bag containing a present, and then whirling pizza dough over my head while everyone oohs and aahs.

First, though, I'll have to buy a decent present. If I'm going to buy anything for a girl, I'll have to get it in Stanhope on the way to the restaurant.

I'll also be paying for a return train ticket, so that's quite a chunk out of my money.

I decide to just tell Dad that I'm going to a mate's party in Stanhope, but that activates his 20 questions sensor.

What mate? Where? Who else will be going? What train will I be back on?

Welcome, All!

I'm a woman of substance – I own a hotel,
With rooms by the hundreds, each taken as well.
Admitted, my guests are all living there free,
But that's not a problem, the treat is on me!
They buzz and they hum as they wing to and fro,
With flowers and insects, my garden's aglow.
So if you should wonder where each of them dwell,
They've all taken lodgings in my Bug Hotel!

Maggie Ingall

Luckily, even a nerd like me does have a few mates at school (in chess and computer club), so it's not beyond the bounds of possibility that one of them might be having a party at a restaurant in Stanhope.

We haggle about the return train until I agree that I'll be back by 10.30 p.m.

Then I ask, very casually, if I can borrow his leather jacket. It's been hanging in the downstairs nook for ages and he only wears it for his occasional trips to the pub.

"You're welcome to borrow it," he says, looking surprised. "But it'll be a bit long in the arms."

I just love the feel and smell of it. I can roll back the sleeves at the cuffs. As I'm trying it on, he does spoil things a bit by telling me it's not real leather.

"Your mum wouldn't like me wearing leather," he remarks, which gives me a warm feeling.

The trouble with asking to borrow the jacket is that it activates Dad's "is there a certain young lady on the horizon?" sensor.

I'm used to heading him off at the pass, though, so I just say, "As if," then slide neatly into, "Shall I make us cocoa?" and he doesn't delve any deeper.

✳   ✳   ✳   ✳

The big night arrives.

I'm feeling pretty good about my plan to turn up at the restaurant, especially as Elinor almost definitely smiled at me earlier today in double history.

I hurry home (dodging Gary, for once) and have a long bath before I get dressed. I've teamed the jacket with a new, neutral-coloured T-shirt and my ripped jeans.

Dad insists on dropping me off at the train station. He presses a ten-pound note into my hand before I get out of the car, but does it quickly, as if he's a spy passing me a memory stick.

"Got your phone?" he checks. "Fully charged? Call me when you get to the restaurant.

"Then call me from Stanhope station, soon as you're homeward bound."

Dad's a full-time fusspot, but I'm used to it.

His final word before he drives off is, "No drinking alcohol, Kev, I mean it."

My intel has uncovered that Elinor's parents are going to be at the restaurant, having a meal downstairs while "the youngsters" party in a function room upstairs.

One thing I'll be doing is arriving fashionably late.

Proceedings start at six-thirty p.m., so I plan to get there by seven. This should also ensure that I don't run into any of my peers on the train to Stanhope.

Not that many of them would recognise me in my jacket, though. It's a whole new Kevin Stevens tonight.

Stanhope is full of Friday evening revellers as I step out of the station and brave the high street.

I've often come here with Dad for clothes shopping and whatnot, but tonight it's different, somehow – there's an end-of-week electrical charge in the air.

I duck into a department store that has late opening. I buy Elinor a strawberry-flavoured lip balm with a matching lipstick and a make-up bag with a zigzaggy pattern.

It should complement the zigzaggy-patterned pencil case I've seen her using.

The lady on the make-up counter asks if I'd like them gift-wrapped at no extra charge, which is great.

The wrapping also has the store logo, so Elinor will know it's good stuff, so that's another bonus.

And so, to Zanzini's. My heart's thumping as a I arrive at the restaurant. Dusk has turned to darkness and the plate-glass sides of the building are lit up.

I text Dad then stand on the other side of the street and do a recce of figures inside the illuminated glass.

Downstairs in Zanzini's, lots of people are tucking into their food at tables. Upstairs, I can plainly see kids milling about, dressed up to the nines.

There's Daisy Harper, Guvinder Singh, and the party girl herself, Elinor. She's wearing a really nice blue dress and wobbling about on big cork-wedged heels.

I don't see Beth – but I do see Gary Hedgeley. He's wearing a chef's apron and a big white hat and plainly acting the big "I am" already. Other kids are hanging off him, laughing.

And suddenly, I can't do it. I can't mosey on in there like a gunslinger in the old west.

I'll be slaughtered by Hedgeley and his posse when they see me slinking into a party I was never invited to, wearing a – let's face it – fake leather jacket two sizes too big.

What had I been thinking?

I hurry away, back towards the train station. I'm really mad now at the money I've wasted trying to prove that I'm something – somebody – I'm not.

The department store is still open so I rush in and mumble about wanting a refund. Thank goodness it's a different woman on the make-up desk.

She refunds my gift receipt without a murmur and I hand over the glittery offering that Elinor Jenkins never knew existed.

✳   ✳   ✳   ✳

When I reach the station, I see it's a whole hour before there's a train back to the village. But even then I'll still be back miles earlier than 10.30 p.m.

When I do get back, I decide, thinking quickly, I won't call Dad for a pick-up.

Instead, I'll go to the village fish and chip shop and eat some greasy comfort food in the park before I go home, then just tell Dad I got a slightly earlier train.

I'll have to make up a load of guff about what a great time I had, but not so great that I was tempted to stay on. It'll be a tricky balancing act, but I'm used to those.

As I'm sitting on the platform with my chin hunkered down in my collar, a figure plonks down on the next bench but one. I recognise her profile and sit up.

"Beth?"

She looks up with a start.

"Kev! What's that you're wearing?"

I wait for her to laugh, but she doesn't. Instead, she slides cautiously on to the end of my bench.

"Don't look at me!" she says crossly, which seems a bit rich, as she's given me a whole stare-fest over the jacket. Anyway, her plea only makes me peer at her harder.

"You've been crying!" I blurt out.

"I don't wish to discuss it," she snaps, folding her bare arms and shivering in her sleeveless spangly dress.

On impulse, I sweep off my jacket and reach across to drape it over her shoulders.

I feel a bit like Sir Walter Raleigh chucking his cloak over a puddle for Elizabeth I.

"Oh. Thanks." She inhales the fabric. "Nice smell. Like your dad's shop. I love going in there." She looks up at me and smiles.

"When I was little, I thought it was like Aladdin's cave."

"It's not real leather," I explain. "But that also means that no cows were harmed to make it.

"So it's not distressed leather, either."

She rolls her eyes.

"You tell terrible jokes."

But at least she got the joke. Elinor Jenkins wouldn't have, that's for sure.

I start to wonder if it's possible that a confident girl like Beth Jones might experience an emotion like panic.

But then, here she is in a sparkly dress, clearly having been crying and clearly having fled the party.

"Beth . . ." I begin.

"Why aren't you at the party?" she asks quickly, getting in her question first.

I confess that I got cold feet.

"After all, I was never formally invited." I pause. "To be honest, they're not really my crowd.

"So – why aren't you there?"

At first I think she's not going to answer me. But after a bit she sniffs.

"Gary Hedgeley is a pig!"

I have to admit, as soon as she says that, a little ping of self-satisfaction goes off in my stomach.

"No argument from me." I nod.

Turns out she promised her folks she'd come back on the train with two other girls she travelled up from the village with.

"But I couldn't stick another minute! Hedgeley called me . . ." her chin trembled ". . . a stick insect! A gangly stick insect! He even did an impression of me walking!"

I bite my lip to stop myself smiling.

She is quite tall, now that I look at her. And slim. But only in a good way.

Gary Hedgeley is an idiot – luckily for me.

"I'm getting chips back in the village," I tell her. "We could share a bag and eat them in the park. If you like."

* * * *

A couple of hours later, as Beth waves to me from the fork that leads to the Willows, I realise that she's heading back to her house still wrapped in Dad's jacket.

I think about calling after her, but only for a second. Instead, I watch her all the way to the bottom of her drive (it's what a gent does) and then I go home.

"You look very pleased with yourself," Dad observes, putting down the evening paper as I slope through the back door. "Why are you so early, though?"

"Party was a bit lame."

Dad's eyes narrow suspiciously.

"Why didn't you call me from the station?"

Boy, he doesn't miss a trick.

"Didn't want to upset our pre-arranged time."

A little jerk of his chin tells me he's not sure whether to believe that, but he'll let it go for now.

"And last but not least, where's my jacket?"

I'm ready for this.

Confidently, I trot out my carefully prepared answer: that I met a fellow villager on the train back and she's borrowed the jacket, temporarily.

"But I'll get it back," I promise happily.

I know Beth will have to see me again to return it. A small part of me even hopes she wore it home deliberately, so she'd have a reason to see me again.

We kissed before she reached the fork in the road. This time, it was a proper first kiss.

I'm well aware that Dad's sensors have picked up my reference to a "she" and are vibrating like crazy.

But instead of asking more questions, he looks at me over his glasses and smiles.

"Fancy some cocoa?"

*   *   *   *

Three things happen after that:

Beth comes round in the morning to the shop, the jacket folded carefully over her arm.

She introduces herself to Dad, who doesn't do anything gross or embarrassing.

In fact, he gives her a free quarter pound of pear drops and we arrange to meet later, in the park, because Venus is going to be out again tonight.

Then, Saturday lunchtime, Dad comes into the back room where I'm finishing my homework and plonks down a dusty box. Inside is this amazing-looking camera.

"My dad got me that when he saw my interest in photography. Thought you might like the use of it." He pauses.

"Or we could go birdwatching some weekend. There's a place near here with some great hides." His eyes shine with enthusiasm.

"I might even capture a great-crested grebe."

I look at the camera. It's not new, but it's still a pretty smart piece of kit – but photography's not really my thing, if I'm being completely honest.

But sounds like it still could be Dad's.

"That sounds great," I say. "And if you ever wanted to go off on your own, to a class or to take some photos, I could, you know, watch the shop.

"Just not for all time," I add hastily.

The thing is, I've found a passion of my own recently that might become something more than a phase. It's not photography, but something like it.

I've taken to sketching a lot in my spare time. My latest one is of a girl in a leather jacket – I've spent quite a lot of time on that one and I'm pretty pleased with it.

I've been thinking on and off for a while about art college. Maybe it's time I gave it serious consideration.

* * * *

The third thing happens on Monday morning.

Over the weekend, I thought long and hard about giving Gary Hedgeley all the wrong answers for his latest maths homework. It was very tempting.

Not only would it give me a lot of satisfaction, it would be sweet payback for how he teased Beth at the party in front of a bunch of kids she didn't know.

But I know that the subtle approach, while satisfying, would only delay the inevitable confrontation.

So when I get on the bus, I stop at his seat and look down at him before pushing his maths book into his hands.

He looks up with a self-satisfied sneer on his face and begins to speak, but I get in first.

"You're on your own from here on in, Gary." Then I walk away, leaving him with his mouth hanging open.

Once his brain's caught up with what just happened, he'll probably get me in a headlock later, but much good it will do him.

I've finally worked out that the only weapon I have against the likes of Gary Hedgeley is not being scared of him any more, and letting him know it.

It's not a massively powerful weapon, true, but I hope it might be enough.

Anyway, Beth will be waiting for me when I get off the bus. She's going to come to my house for tea, and I'm trusting that Dad will behave and not do anything embarrassing.

After that, we're going to the titchy village cinema to see some girly film I don't really fancy, but I'm happy enough to give it a go if it means spending time with her.

And next time, I get to pick.

Then afterwards, we're getting chips on the way home. ∎

Streatley, Berkshire

Lose yourself in the picturesque surroundings of Streatley and its neighbouring village Goring-on-Thames, linked by a bridge built in 1923. Prior to this, a simpler timber bridge spanned the river.

Both villages are steeped in history, being mentioned in the Domesday Book, and back in 1932 the remains of a Saxon warrior were discovered by local man Alfred Woodage, along with an iron spearhead and knife .

There are trails aplenty for keen walkers wishing to explore the Areas of Outstanding Natural Beauty, from walks taking just an hour or two to much longer hikes – the Swan's Way follows a bridle path and covers 65 miles.

Those who prefer to view the countryside from two wheels will have much to see, while serious cyclists are drawn to the tough gradient of Streatley Hill.

The area is also home to one of the oldest rowing regattas, which began in 1888. Basildon Park also featured in scenes from the popular "Downton Abbey" series. Of course, the Swan hostelry – once owned by Danny La Rue – has its own claim to fame in that it's mentioned in "The Wind In The Willows".

Into The Sunset

by Patsy Goodsir

SELINA crawled along the narrow country road, rounded a bend and there it was, in the distance, the distinct red roof. Her journey was almost over.

She was overwhelmed with emotion: sadness, because her great-aunt Primrose was no longer there; excitement, because it now belonged to her; and apprehension, because she wasn't sure what to do with it. Her life was in the city with Toby.

Suddenly her old car coughed, spluttered and lost its voice. She banged the steering wheel in temper.

"I don't believe it. What now?"

She picked up her mobile. No signal. Maybe she should walk to the cottage. She'd arranged for the landline to be reconnected. But who was she going to phone?

She stepped out of the car and shaded her eyes from the midday sun. Behind her, sheep ripped at the ample grass, while a couple of horses swished tails and dozed beneath an old oak tree. She daren't tell Toby – he would chastise her for being so stupid.

"Got a problem?"

Selina turned to see a tall young man in a checked shirt clear a fence like a deer. A black and white collie greeted her, wagging his tail.

"Stay down, Max."

Selina felt such a fool.

"I'm afraid I've run out of petrol. And it has to be today when my car is loaded to the hilt."

Max's master smiled.

"We were watching you from the top field. Just up there checking the sheep. Thought something must be wrong."

Selina nodded.

"I'm heading for the red-roofed cottage you can see in the distance."

"Aha, Primrose's place. You must be Selina."

It was Selina's turn to smile.

Illustration by Mandy Murray.

"News travels fast."

"I'm Scott – my old man farms this land. I've been out in Australia for a few years, but it was time to come home to let Dad take it a bit easier.

"Give me five minutes, and I'll come back with the Land-Rover and tow you to the cottage. I've got to go into town later so I'll bring you back some petrol. How does that sound?"

Selina heaved a huge sigh of relief.

"That would be wonderful. Thank you so much."

"OK, see you in five. Come on, Max." Scott set off at a trot with Max in hot pursuit.

Selina sat down on the grass and cast her gaze to the distant cottage, remembering childhood days of sitting beneath the apple tree with Primrose.

Funny to think that Scott had been growing up a few fields away. She'd probably seen him loads of times, in the distance or passing by on the tractor with his dad.

Cotton-wool clouds melted into oblivion, leaving a brilliant azure blue that reflected on the shimmering sea. She was surrounded by birdsong.

The sound of the approaching Land-Rover made her scramble to her feet. Scott did a quick U-turn and reversed to Selina's car. And so the final part of the journey began.

"Here we are." Scott pulled up at the green-painted gate. The apple tree was in full blossom, but the garden was overgrown.

"Oh, goodness, look at all those weeds!" Selina said as she jumped down from the Land-Rover.

"Don't go buying all that expensive stuff at garden centres. I can bring you something from the farm that will shift them."

"Thank you. That's very kind."

"My pleasure."

He had one of those winning smiles. Selina's gaze lingered on his suntanned face. Bright blue eyes sparkled behind dark lashes.

"Right, I'll give you a hand in with some of this and then I'll be off. Got a cow calving and I need to keep an eye on this one."

It was strange, opening the front door of Fern Cottage and knowing Primrose was no longer there to greet her with a welcome cup of tea and a freshly baked scone.

The front room was a place where time stood still. A lovely window seat gave you a view of Scott's farm. The front-facing window looked out to the sea.

The chintz-covered armchair lay empty, and a few salty tears slid down her cheeks as an image of her aunt quietly reading beneath her fringed standard lamp filled her mind.

Selina wasn't sure she'd ever part with any of the books. She pulled out two or three and sank into the comfy old sofa.

* * * *

"Hello!"

Selina woke, her heart pounding and saw Scott standing in the doorway.

"Sorry. I did knock but got no reply. Just wondered, did you want to come into town with me in case there's anything you need?"

"Oh, I didn't realise I was so tired. I must have nodded off. OK, yes, thanks. That would be great."

* * * *

"Let me make you a cup of coffee or tea for helping me out today," Selina said when they got back.

Scott smiled and followed Selina into the cottage.

"Not sure what I'm going to do with this place, Scott," she said. "Might rent it out, might sell it. If I could afford to, I'd like to keep it for myself, but a lot of my work is based in London."

"Well, if you decide to hang on to the place, I can keep on top of the weeds for you."

Curled up in bed that evening, Selina found herself thinking about Scott and his kind offer to look after her garden.

She reached for a book about birds that lay on the bedside table and caught a piece of paper that fell from between the pages.

It was a handwritten note from Primrose.

Darling Selina,

No-one understood when I left the city to come to Fern Cottage, but that's because they're not like me. I know you will be uncertain what to do, but please don't make any hasty decisions because there is a magic about this place you won't find anywhere else.

This book will help you recognise all the different birds that will become your friends. And once you've seen one of the spectacular sunsets, you will never want to leave.

The Morrisons who farm nearby are a delight, especially Scott, who has recently returned to take over. Never be too proud to ask their advice on anything. I have no doubt at all that you will do what's right for you and for this special place.

With all my love,
Primrose.

✻   ✻   ✻   ✻

The light was flashing on the phone base. Selina was sleeping so well at Fern Cottage she hadn't even heard it ring.

"Hi, honey!" Toby's voice boomed down the phone. "Should be with you this evening. Can't give a time and I hope I don't get lost."

Selina felt her pulse race. She'd better cook something nice if Toby was arriving.

"How's things?" a voice shouted as Selina made a selection from the herb corner in the garden. It was Scott in the Land-Rover.

Selina smiled.

"Everything is fine. My boyfriend is driving up tonight."

"OK – have a good evening."

Selina was too busy to notice the disappointment in Scott's face.

She guessed Toby would arrive around six-thirty p.m. so timed her menu for around seven. It was a small but practical kitchen, painted a lovely sunshine yellow. A happy kitchen.

Everything was on target, so she'd better sort herself out and brush her hair. It was the perfect evening, calm and bright. Toby would see Fern Cottage at its best.

She waved to Scott as he drove by when she was picking some flowers to put in a vase.

The base light on the landline was flashing.

"Hi, darling, you're going to kill me, but I can't make it. I'm going to have to work late tonight. See you soon. I'll try to make it tomorrow. Love you."

Selina wandered into the garden, unexpectedly close to tears. She didn't know what she felt. She opened the gate, needing to walk off some pent-up emotions.

It was a beautiful evening. The cottage seemed to glow in the evening sun. Her thoughts turned to her aunt Primrose. What on earth would she have said?

"Pull yourself together" was a fairly safe bet. She was in the process of doing that when Scott's Land-Rover appeared round the bend.

He drew up alongside her.

"Hi, what a lovely evening. Where's the boyfriend?"

Selina felt her face flush.

"He can't make it." She cleared her throat. "Scott, have you eaten, because I have a chicken galliano that is going to be wasted."

"I have no idea what that is, but I'll give it a try. Is it OK if Max comes?"

A black and white head bobbed up in the back of the Land-Rover.

"Of course."

"Hop in, then – you might as well get a lift back before that chicken spoils."

$*$ $*$ $*$ $*$

"Now I'm going to repay that wonderful meal," Scott said, pushing his plate away. "Then I have something to show you."

He scooped up the plates and took them to the kitchen, washed up and put the dishes on the drying rack.

"Do you have anything sensible for your feet?"

"I have walking boots in the back of the car."

"Best get them on, then – but we'll take the Land-Rover some of the way."

Soon they were bumping along a rutted track. They reached a gate and Scott switched off the engine.

"It's on foot from here."

Selina didn't question him. He seemed very enthusiastic, so whatever it was she was sure it would be something worth seeing.

The track soon became a sliding, slithering path down a steep banking. Scott steadied Selina's balance with a strong arm till they eventually hit a piece of glorious silver sand.

To get over some rocks he again took her hand, but this time he held on. He gazed at the slipping sun.

"Come on." He broke into a trot and Selina began to laugh.

"Hey, I can't keep up with you."

"Yes, you can."

Finally, Scott slowed his pace.

"OK. What do you think?"

Before them stood an old cottage with a red tin roof. A sturdy wooden bench sat beneath the right-hand window. He pulled her up the banking and nodded towards the setting sun.

"Just in time."

It was the most beautiful sunset Selina had ever seen. The sky was a deep burnt orange and the sun like a giant peach.

"What is this place, Scott?" she asked softly.

"Just an old bothy – hardly anyone knows about it. It's not exactly easy to get to, but worth it, don't you think?"

Selina was speechless. She had visited exotic places all over the world, but nothing quite had the magic of this place.

The silhouettes of busy oystercatchers, burrowing in the sand, enhanced the strip of gold sweeping across the inky black water.

The only sound came from the ebbing tide, dragging her skirts across the rolling sands.

"Any walkers can use this place, but they're few and far between. Max and I come down here a lot." Scott gave Selina a wink and patted Max's head.

They sat outside on the bench until the medallion of molten gold had slipped behind the distant hills and the burnt orange sky became ruby red.

They talked about their school days, their ambitions. In fact, Selina found herself talking like she'd never talked before.

She soon discovered that Scott had often sat with Primrose in her garden and had similar chats.

"Primrose had an amazing mind and a wicked sense of humour." Scott laughed.

"I think you knew her much better than I did, Scott," Selina admitted regretfully. "I never got much time to visit her, especially over the last few years.

"But she often wrote the most wonderful letters to me, telling me about her life at Fern Cottage.

"Gardening, weaving, spinning, felting, writing. It seems she was always busy doing something."

＊　　＊　　＊　　＊

Although Toby's lack of appearance was a disappointment, Scott had truly saved the day. Selina woke the next morning feeling happy and relaxed.

She sat at her laptop. All sorts of new ideas sprang into her head. The motivation she'd found so lacking seemed to be returning in torrents.

A loud rap at the door, followed by a familiar voice, tore Selina away from her design, inspired by last night's sunset.

"Hi! I finally made it." It was Toby, bearing the most enormous bouquet of roses.

"I wasn't sure if I was on the right road, but a local yokel pointed me in the right direction. I think he lives just across the fields. He appeared out of a field with his dog."

The word "yokel" annoyed Selina, but she said nothing.

"So what do you fancy doing? I hope there's somewhere decent for a pint."

Selina sighed. Her mind went back to the previous evening and that wonderful sunset. Sharing it with Scott had felt very comfortable.

She had to stick to the word "comfortable". Another word ricocheted through her head, but she daren't let herself even think it.

"Let's sit outside," Selina suggested, and went to make coffee.

They sat beneath the apple tree. The moment should have been perfect.

"There's a bit of a pong around here." Toby screwed up his nose and swatted a fly away. "Probably those cows. So what have you decided? Are you going to sell the place or rent it out? It should fetch a decent amount of money."

It irritated Selina immensely that Toby hadn't even taken a look round the beautiful garden that she had already put some effort into tidying up, or Fern Cottage itself, which exuded so much charm.

She felt it almost a slight to Aunt Primrose's memory.

"I haven't decided anything. It's far too soon to make decisions like that. Besides, I like it here."

Their exchange was interrupted by the sound of a vehicle hammering up the road at speed. It ground to an abrupt halt and Scott jumped out.

"So sorry to interrupt your day, but I really need your help. My parents are out and it's our stockman's weekend off. My mare has got herself caught in the fence.

"I need someone to steady her just in case she starts struggling. She's got a lovely temperament, but can be a bit silly sometimes. I'll only need to cut one wire and she'll be free."

"I'm not much cop around horses," Toby admitted.

"You're not, but I am. I'll just grab my boots." Selina raced inside.

All three headed back towards Scott's farm. A beautiful liver chestnut mare stood with her head low, her foreleg tangled between two wires which had tightened.

"Her name's Chasca. If you could just hold her head and talk to her while I try to cut her free."

Selina took hold of Chasca's headcollar.

"Whoa, girl. What a beautiful name. What a beautiful girl."

Chasca nickered softly. Selina held on tight as the mare flinched when Scott started the task of releasing her from the wire with a pair of strong wire cutters. Toby stood watching, unsure what to do.

It didn't take long to free her.

"I'll walk her around a little bit till you see if she's sound, Scott."

Toby stood, surplus to requirements, as Selina walked the mare towards Scott and trotted her away from him.

"She looks pretty sound to me, don't you think?"

Scott scratched his head and a big grin formed on his face, then he let out a big sigh of relief.

"I think you're right, but I'll take her back to the steading and hose down that leg."

"You can't leave the Land-Rover here." Selina grinned. "Toby and I will meet you at the steading. I'm sure I can handle one of these."

With that, Selina got herself behind the wheel.

* * * *

Over the next few days, Selina and Toby relaxed at the cottage, went out for walks and ate in a quaint old pub just a few miles away.

Occasionally Selina saw Scott checking out the top fields with Max and wondered if Chasca had got over her encounter with the fence.

By Tuesday night, Toby had headed back to London.

"See you soon, then. Let me know if you want Jamie Johnson to come and give you a valuation. He owes me a favour."

The word "valuation" didn't sit well with Selina – it just sounded like a betrayal of her aunt's wishes.

The location and the beautiful garden had inspired all sorts of new ideas; Selina felt as though she had come alive, far from the hassle of traffic and noise.

She could see herself with a small studio in the garden. Inspiration was all around her: scents, smells, birdsong.

She had just washed up her evening meal dishes when Max came running into her kitchen, panting as always. She expected Scott to follow, but he didn't, so she walked outside.

"Hey, Chasca has come to say thank you."

Scott sat astride a big chestnut gelding, holding a lead rein to the beautiful mare.

"You did say you could ride, didn't you?"

"Gosh, yes, but not for ages."

Scott laughed.

"Don't worry, she'll look after you and her leg is fine. I've even brought you a hard hat, so there's no excuse".

Selina felt she'd lost the argument. She pulled on her boots and took the reins from Scott.

"I'll just need to make sure I don't fall off, as I suspect I might never hear the end of it."

Together they entered a nearby field. There was something about the creak of a saddle, the sound of hooves on the grass and the occasional happy snort.

Oh, how wonderful it was, just covering the ground and enjoying everything around. The field sloped steeply and soon Selina found herself riding Chasca along the beach, in pursuit of Scott on Jupiter.

The wind raced through her hair as sea and sand leapt in protest. Nothing had ever matched this moment, and then it came into sight, that old tin-roofed bothy, slumbering at the foot of the hills and at one with the approaching sunset.

"Race you there!" Scott shouted.

"Oh, that was just fabulous." Selina pulled Chasca up and slapped her velvet neck. "She's amazing, Scott, isn't she?"

"Yes, she is, and she was born and raised on the farm. She's a very special lady. A bit like someone else I know."

Selina loved the terms of endearment Scott used. He was possibly the most kind and caring person she had ever met. No wonder Primrose had taken him to her heart.

The horses stood obediently as their riders climbed the banking to the bothy bench.

"Just in time," Scott said as he nodded towards the sinking sun.

He held out his hand to stop Selina sliding on the banking. He held it tightly and she made no attempt to pull it away.

London seemed a million miles away from this special place, and as the sun finally disappeared Selina knew that she was about to make a decision that would have pleased Primrose.

The old cliché of riding off into the sunset had never made more sense. ■

Wandering Winnie

by Patricia Belford

MAY was sitting in the back yard, reheeling her brother's boots while the younger children played in the sunshine. It was her day off from her job at the hospital and she was looking after her sister, Winnie, and the twins, Alfie and Tom, who were two.

Her little brothers, playing quietly together, were no trouble, but four-year-old Winnie needed watching. The bolt on the gate was worn loose, and she sometimes managed to get out into the street.

It was a breezy day and the shirts May had washed earlier were dancing on the line. She took the first boot off the old iron last and with a sharp knife trimmed round the rubber heel.

She was just starting on the other boot when her friend, Rosie, who was passing, called over the wall.

"Hey, May, are you coming to the dance tonight?"

May, pliers in hand, shook her head.

"I can't, Rosie, Ma's working late at the bakery and I've promised to stay at home with the children."

"But you couldn't come last week, either. There'll be plenty of lads to dance with. I'm going with Cyril."

May couldn't help feeling a pang of envy.

It was not that she actually fancied any of the local lads, but it would be good to have someone special, even if it was just for a walk in the park. Surely one day, she thought, she would meet someone.

"It's a shame! You work hard at the hospital and you should be having some fun," Rosie said as she went on her way.

May was nearly seventeen and the eldest of six. When her father had died over a year ago, her mother had been forced to take on the extra

Set in
the
1920s

Illustration by Kirk Houston.

evening work at the baker's to make ends meet.

However tired May was after her shift at the hospital, she knew it was her duty to help with the little ones. Her ma depended on her.

She began to rip the worn heel off the boot with the pliers. Her pa had been a cobbler and May had loved watching him work when she was small.

Money was short, and without May's efforts, her brothers might have had to walk barefoot to school.

May was fitting the boot on the last when she realised that she hadn't seen or heard Winnie for some time. She glanced round in a panic. Alfie and Tom were in a corner of the yard with an old wooden lorry, making "pip pip" noises, but of Winnie there was no sign.

"Did you see where our Winnie went?" she asked, but they just raised their identical faces, shook their heads and returned to their game.

"Right." May sighed. "Stay here in the yard while I go and look for her!"

She ran out of the gate, along the street then round the corner to the next one, but there was no sign of her sister.

May hurried along the adjoining streets, glancing round for the sight of her little sister in her blue dress, getting more and more worried because she couldn't leave the twins alone for much longer.

She saw a coal cart trundle past the end of the road and tears sprang into her eyes as a terrifying thought flashed through her mind.

Winnie might have been run over!

* * * *

Police Constable Robbie Trent was enjoying the warm sunshine as he walked his beat. He had already waylaid two young lads who were habitual truants and had marched them into the junior school.

Now he called into the butcher's for some boiled ham, the regular order to which he and his colleagues treated themselves on a Friday for their midday break.

He stowed the package in his pocket, for his sergeant did not allow his men to carry parcels when in uniform.

The old church clock struck twelve and Robbie had just decided to take a last walk past the shops on the other side of the street when he spotted a small girl, all alone as she skipped along the pavement.

When he reached her she was playing in a puddle, crouching down and dabbling her hands in the water, laughing as she splashed herself.

As Robbie bent towards her, she stood up and dipped one foot in the puddle.

"Now, little girl, you're going spoil that pretty dress and those nice boots."

When he looked closer, he saw that the dress was faded and patched and the boots were split and badly scuffed, probably passed down from an older child. Well, that was about normal for these parts.

"Where's your ma?"

The child shrugged her shoulders and made another splash.

"What's your name, love?"

There was still no reply. Robbie glanced around. The street was quiet and no-one seemed to be searching for a lost child. He tried again.

"My name's Robbie," he said. "Are you going to tell me yours?"

"Winnie."

At last he was getting somewhere. He held out his hand.

"Well, Winnie, I think we should go for a little walk to keep you safe, because your ma will be looking for you. Shall we go and get a cup of tea?"

The little girl stood up and smiled, then she took his hand.

"You took your time, young Robbie," Sergeant Brown said, when the pair walked into the station. "The kettle's been boiling these last ten minutes. And who's this?"

"Winnie," Robbie said. "I found her wandering in the street. She hasn't told me her other name."

"I daresay someone'll come to report her missing before long. Bring her in the back with us so we can keep an eye on her."

In a few minutes the tea was mashed and Archie, the other constable, was stirring the big brown teapot. Robbie sat Winnie at the table in the small back room and gave her a slice of bread and butter and a mug of milky tea.

The three men shared the ham between themselves and had begun to discuss United's chances in tomorrow's match when a small voice piped up.

"I have meat on my bread at home!"

The policemen looked at each other. Sergeant Brown cut his last slice of ham in two and laid a piece on the child's plate.

"She's a cheeky little scrap, isn't she?" he said. "Reminds me of our Annie when she were a nipper."

Winnie ate her bread and ham with relish, then got down from her chair.

"Get after her, Robbie. We don't want her going missing again."

Robbie drained his tea and hurried after the child, just as a middle-aged woman with a shopping basket pushed opened the door of the station.

She had come to hand in a purse she had found in the street. As Robbie took her particulars, the woman spotted Winnie.

"What's she doing here?" she asked.

Robbie stared.

"You know her?"

"Seen her about. She lives round our way."

"Give me her address, then."

The woman shook her head.

"Nay, I don't know the address but it's one of those streets off Shepherd's Lane."

"Best walk her up there, PC Trent," Sergeant Brown said. "And mind you hand her over to her family and take the full particulars."

Holding Winnie's hand firmly, Robbie walked along the street and turned the corner by the junior school.

"Now, Winnie," he said, "you'll have to show me which is your house."

Winnie just nodded and smiled at him. They plodded on, down one cobbled street after another. No-one they met seemed to know Winnie, but as they were passing the sixth street, Robbie noticed a young woman hurrying along the pavement.

"There!" Winnie shouted.

The woman ran towards them. She had the same red-gold hair as the child and little curls bounced round her head as she ran.

"Winnie! Where have you been?"

She bent to give Winnie a hug then gazed up at Robbie and he saw tears of relief spilling down her cheeks.

"I've been looking everywhere for her!"

"I found the little lass by the shops. Don't take on, Mrs . . .?"

"Scott. Miss Scott. May. Winnie's my sister. She must have slipped out while my back was turned. Our mother's at work. I've had to get a neighbour to keep an eye on the little ones."

She brushed her tears away.

"Thank you for finding her," she said.

Robbie smiled.

"We kept her safe, miss. She's even had her lunch in the police station!"

"I had meat!" Winnie announced, giving the policeman a huge grin.
"Aye, she told us she has meat on her bread at home," Robbie said.
"Not very often. You're a lucky girl!" May said.
She looked at Robbie and her smile echoed her small sister's.
Robbie felt his heart lurch.
"Now, I'll see you both home safely," he said. "Just show me the way."
Winnie clung to his hand and gave her other to May, then she skipped along between them.
"Where did you find her?" May asked, relaxing.
"She was by the shopping parade, dipping her boots in a puddle," Robbie said. "Her feet are soaking."
Winnie stopped and lifted her foot.
"Never mind, Winnie, I'll stick a patch on them tomorrow."
The policeman was staring at her.
"You?"
"Our dad was a cobbler. He died, but I used to watch him work and I mend all our boots and shoes."
She glanced down at the policeman's enormous polished boots.
"But I wouldn't know how to tackle yours!"
They were still laughing as they turned the corner into May's street.

* * * *

The next day was Saturday. After finishing the early shift, May hurried home. Her mother was not working, so she was looking forward to having a peaceful afternoon cutting up an old dress.
It was a pretty green with a design of small spots and there was enough material to remake it.
As she turned the corner of her street, she was surprised to see the policeman who had found Winnie coming out of their back yard.
"Good day!" he said. "I've been to see your mother. The sergeant wanted a few more particulars as she wasn't in when we brought the little lass home yesterday."
"Thank you again for your help," May said. "Mother's going to the school on Monday to ask if they can take Winnie a bit earlier than usual. At least it might tire her out and stop her wandering."
"Winnie the Wanderer! That's a good name for her. Your ma said you work at the hospital, Miss Scott?"
"It's May, remember? Yes," she said, "but it's my day off tomorrow."
"And I'm Robbie. It's my day off tomorrow, too," he said.
He went rather pink and took a deep breath.
"May . . . I wonder, would you care to go for a walk in the park?"
May smiled.
"Thank you. I'd love to."
"I'll call for you at two o'clock," he said. "We'll go and listen to the band playing."
"Two o'clock!" May said. "I'd better go in now, and help Ma."
"Aye, and watch that little sister of yours," Robbie said. "We don't want her wandering off again!" ∎

Vintage Cleaning Tips from the "Friend"

Olive oil

WE usually want to remove oil and grease during a cleaning session, but in the right place and at the right time, oils and fats can also serve to banish or prevent grime and other stains from blemishing wood, metal and even textiles.

Wooden bowls and serving platters are fashionable again, so a spring-cleaning tip from 1961 could come in handy: "Lightly-polished wooden articles, such as salad bowls, should be wiped over with a slightly-moist cloth, then rubbed dry. Give an occasional rub with a trace of olive oil to preserve the wood."

Not only does it make a tasty salad dressing, but a little olive oil can help you clean up afterwards, too!

It can also brighten up your surroundings – that is, if you possess parchment lampshades. In 1966, the "Friend" advised that these "should be rubbed gently with a small cloth dipped in olive oil. Vellum shades also require this treatment".

Want to keep that hard-won shine on metalwork? Another 1966 tip suggests, "After polishing brass rub over with a little furniture cream or olive oil, finishing off with a soft cloth."

But olive oil wasn't only a household help in the 1960s. Back in 1882, a piano-making reader shared a method for removing finger-marks from and restoring lustre to highly polished but much-defaced furniture:

"Wash off the finger-marks with a cloth – or, better, a chamois skin – wet with cold water, then rub the surface with a nice sweet oil mixed with half its quantity of turpentine. A liberal rubbing of this mixture will reward your labours."

Sweet oil was another name for olive oil at that time.

Oil's well . . .! ■

Lipstick On The Ceiling

—— by Pamela Ormondroyd ——

I 'LL never forget you, Vince. Never!"

"Oh, Lottie – dear, sweet Lottie."

Vincent Bryce smiled and took Lottie's face in his hands. The pair stared into each other's eyes and for a split second, Lottie was sure that the handsome young airman was trying to tell her something.

But then Vince sighed deeply and seemed pained, as if he just couldn't find the right words, and pulled her to him, whereupon Lottie laid her head on his shoulder and wept.

They'd only known each other a few months but the pair had hit it off immediately, not giving a thought to the inevitable day of parting. But now that day had come and it was unbearably hard.

Lottie lifted her damp cheeks from Vince's camel jacket.

"Even if I live till I'm a hundred, Vince, I promise I'll never, ever forget you . . ."

* * * *

And so it was that today, 75 years later, Lottie Warburton meant to honour her promise.

She and her extended family were celebrating the lady's one hundredth birthday in the revamped saloon of the Red Lion public house in the centre of town.

It was a striking listed building and always popular with punters. The staff had gone to great lengths to make Lottie's birthday party very special indeed, providing a splendid buffet on a long, nicely decorated table that filled a lounge decked with bright balloons and bunting.

Lottie sat back in her chair at the head of the table, pleased that the old place still retained the old flagstone floor and cosy recesses which she had known in her youth.

Pleasant conversation surrounded her; familiar voices of her extended family, of whom she was immensely proud.

Illustration by David Young.

She closed her eyes fleetingly, revelling in the present love and warmth, and her mind drifted back 75 years to the summer of 1943 when the Red Lion bar was crowded and noisy and the Yanks were in town.

*   *   *   *

"Hey, just come and take a look at this, Lottie."

The pretty barmaid with the ruby red lips put down her tea towel for a moment and hurried to the window facing the street.

"He'll be one of the new Yanks from the base, I bet," Joe continued. "Well, if he manages to steer that bundle of rust into the back yard without falling off, it'll be a miracle."

Lottie watched as the young serviceman grappled nervously with his bicycle, which was hurtling along the steep cobbled lane that led down to the Red Lion public house at the bottom.

The lane was already notorious for accidents, most of which involved young Americans from the nearby airbase who, in the main, had never ridden an antiquated English contraption known as a "sit up and beg" before.

Lottie put her hand to her mouth as the bike suddenly veered to the right and out of view. A few seconds later a crashing sound was heard.

"He's landed!" Joe chuckled as he strained his neck to see out of the side window. Lottie, meanwhile, raced past him and hurried outside to find a young blond-haired chap sitting in a heap, looking quite bemused as the wheels of his bicycle kept spinning.

"Oh, my goodness, are you hurt?"

The young man, red-faced and gasping a little, waved his hand.

"Hardly at all, ma'am, though I fear the bike is a write-off." He struggled up and Lottie noticed that he had scraped his hand quite badly.

"Come inside," she said. "I'll clean you up."

In the pub kitchen she found a bowl and poured some warm water into it. Then she took a clean tea towel, dipped it in the bowl, and gently proceeded to remove small pieces of grit from the wound.

"I tried to pull the brakes as taut as they'd go but it didn't make any difference," the young man said, wincing a little.

Lottie shook her head.

"I don't know where they get those bikes from but they don't seem at all roadworthy," she said. "You're from the base, then? New, are you?"

The young man nodded.

"Yes, ma'am. Came down from Liverpool at the weekend. Thought I'd explore the area a bit. Check out the Lion, my crew said. Best place in town. Only they never told me it was over four miles away."

Lottie smiled.

"There you are," she said. "All done."

The serviceman jumped up and bowed.

"Thank you, ma'am. Much obliged. I'm Vince, by the way, Vince Bryce, radio operator, from Chicago, Illinois."

"Well, Vince Bryce from Chicago, Illinois, welcome to the Red Lion. You're only just in time for a quick half, though, I'm afraid, because we close at two p.m. Maybe if you find yourself a decent bike you'll get here earlier next time."

And the pair looked at each other and grinned, a friendship already formed.

He was a good-looking, pleasant fellow, she thought to herself as he went outside to inspect the damage. But he seemed so terribly young.

Too young and innocent to be bravely risking his life in one of the massive bombers that frequently flew over her roof at night, carrying its deadly cargo. That was why Lottie always went out of her way to help make the new airmen feel at home.

To be always patient, cheerful and kind.

"I can lend you another bike to ride back on, if you like," she said, joining Vince in the yard. "We have a few spares in the shed. And I can ride part of the way to show you the shortcut."

She offered her hand and Vince shook it warmly.

"And I'm Lottie, Lottie Warburton, barmaid from the Red Lion. Pleased to meet you."

*   *   *   *

"So, how long you been working at the Lion, then, Lottie?"

Lottie and Vince had met up a few weeks later and she had taken him on a country bike ride, showing him a few of the local attractions: an old ruined priory, a hidden lake, a copse of wild strawberries.

The two of them got on well, both being easy-going and sharing a love of the countryside.

"Not long, and I'm only part-time," she said, as they rested by a stile. "I help on the family farm most of the time. I'll take you up there one day. Mum and Dad would be pleased to meet you, Vince.

"I'm happy there but it can be a bit lonely sometimes, so when Joe asked if I'd like to help out at the Lion, I jumped at the chance."

"I've heard it can get quite rowdy with our lot sometimes," Vince remarked.

"Oh, yes, but it's mostly good-natured. It's good to see the boys letting their hair down now and again."

It was a beautiful day. Fields dotted with yellow and gold, birds in song and apple blossom drifting like confetti in the slight summer breeze. Vince sat back on his saddle and looked about him.

"Gee, I never seen such beauty, not for a long time," he said. "Where I come from you have to travel for hours to see anything quite like this. Thank you for showing it to me."

Lottie smiled, her bright red lipstick gleaming in the sunlight.

"A pleasure, Vince," she said. "All part of the service."

He chuckled and put his foot on the pedal. He travelled a short distance and then pulled up and turned.

"You and Joe," he said. "Are you an item?"

Lottie laughed.

"Oh, no. Joe's my cousin." She paused for a moment. "I have got a special boy in my life, though, Vince. He's called Ronnie. He's in the Army. North Africa."

"Oh, well, if we mean to be honest with each other, then I have a special girl, too," Vince said, seeming quite relieved. "Miriam, back home in Chicago. We write as much as we can, though the post is pretty poor."

"Well, I'm glad we've cleared that up," Lottie said, smiling. "So we can still be good friends, can't we?"

"We sure can." Vince smiled back then and pressed hard on his pedal. She watched as he rode a little more confidently along the narrow lane.

* * * *

And so began a gentle, uncomplicated relationship between Vince and Lottie. They were good pals and soul mates, mostly cycling or enjoying the odd picnic. Lottie kept her promise and also took Vince to meet her parents on the farm, where he was made most welcome.

Sometimes, however, weeks would pass before they could meet up at all, when there was "something big" on and the skies filled night after night with loud flying monsters.

Lottie would lie awake then, her heart in her mouth, the house vibrating with the thunderous drone, willing the men to return safely.

There were the inevitable sad occasions, of course, when planes were lost and friends did not return, and when the atmosphere in the Lion would be subdued for days.

Yet, when things went well and good news broke, the walls of the pub resounded with laughter and loud banter and the pipes would almost run dry.

The summer months passed and suddenly Vince's run of missions had come to an end and he was granted leave to return to the States.

Joe organised a huge party at the pub which ran on into the early hours. As dawn broke, some of the US airmen pulled the tables together and stood on them. Using paint and chalk and anything else that came to hand, they drew their initials and other missives and reminders on the lounge ceiling, so they wouldn't be forgotten.

"Lend us your lipstick, Lottie." And then Vince was hauled aloft on a pal's shoulders and he wrote her name and his in bright ruby red.

* * * *

"Are you enjoying yourself, Mum?" Wendy, Lottie's daughter, sat down and placed an arm around her shoulder.

"Wonderful," Lottie said. "Best day ever, love."

Wendy smiled. She had a good idea why her mother had chosen the Red Lion for her one hundredth birthday party. Many a time she had listened to Lottie's tales of her war years and her time working at the pub, and Wendy always felt there was more to it than Lottie let on.

* * * *

Only Lottie knew the full story. Of the precious night before Vince went back to the States, when she realised, for the first time, she had fallen in love with him.

And she was certain that he had felt the same; the way he had looked at her that night, the way his lips had trembled though the words just hadn't come.

Yet, when she thought about it afterwards in the cold light of day, she knew that a serious romance between them could never have worked.

It was a different era, an unreal, unstable world where people latched on to a little happiness in order just to get through each day.

And the pull on Vince to get back to his own world was as strong as the hold on Lottie of her own family and country.

They had exchanged letters briefly, though, and she had sent her good wishes when Vince and Miriam were wed. But then correspondence had dwindled as they both knew it would.

Yet Lottie would never forget him.

She stood and cut her birthday cake and, as she raised a glass of champagne, no-one heard her whisper.

"I kept my promise, Vince. I told you I would."

And she looked up at the names of the brave bomber crews, now polished and preserved for posterity, a vital piece of history, shining beneath the light of the chandelier.

And she drank a toast to one very special airman who had climbed on to a beer-stained table all those years before and written her name with lipstick on the ceiling. ■

Know Your Onions

Illustration by Mandy Dixon.

by Alyson Hilbourne

SUE pulled the tray of brownies from the oven and put them on the cooling rack before starting the washing up. Through the kitchen window she saw Tony collect a hoe and spade from the shed. He leaned them against the back wall and called in the open kitchen door.

"I'm off to the allotment!"

"OK. Is everything ready for the show?"

"Ha!" Tony grunted and picked up his tools before slamming the back gate.

Sue rolled her eyes. It was the same every year before the village show.

"Really," she muttered. "You'd think it was Chelsea or Hampton Court the way he carries on."

Five minutes later, she finished the washing up and cut two slices of brownie, which she put on a plate. Then she slipped out the back door and went through into her neighbour's garden.

"Cooee! Only me," she called as she stood at the open kitchen door.

"Come in," Evelyn said. "Excuse the mess."

"Oh, blackberry and apple, and what's this? Strawberry? Rhubarb?" Sue looked at the jam jars on the table, the labels spread out and the big black pan bubbling away on the hob.

A wasp buzzed at the window, drawn by the smell of jam and now unable to get out again.

Evelyn grinned.

"The old standard, blackberry and apple. I've already made strawberry and I'm trying rhubarb and ginger this year."

"I'm impressed," Sue said, nodding.

"You could do it. You make marmalade. Jam is no different," Evelyn told her.

"Ah, but why make it when I know my neighbour will give me some?" Sue said with a grin.

Evelyn burst out laughing.

"Get away with you," she said.

Sue and Evelyn had been friends for years. Their children had gone to school together, they'd babysat for each other and they'd put the world to rights over endless cups of tea and coffee.

"I'm not disturbing you?" Sue asked.

"No, especially if one of those brownies has my name on it. I'll put the kettle on, shall I?

"I just have to keep an eye on this pan until it reaches setting point." Evelyn filled the kettle at the sink and turned back to Sue.

"To be honest, it's nice to see somebody happy. Phil has just gone off to the allotments with a face that would curdle milk."

Sue grinned.

"I had more or less the same. Tony grunted as he went off with his tools. Communication seems to have been put on hold for the village show season."

"What's he entering this year?" Evelyn asked, as she filled the teapot with boiling water.

"Oh, I daren't ask," Sue said. "Classified information. He'd have to shoot me if he told me."

Evelyn grinned.

"They're like children, aren't they?"

"Worse than children," Sue agreed.

Evelyn brought mugs and milk to the table and stirred the tea. She poured for them both and Sue pushed the plate of brownies across towards Evelyn.

"Mmm, these are so good," Evelyn said, licking crumbs from her lips. "Are you entering these in the show? I want the recipe."

"Huh! So you can beat me?" Sue asked and both women laughed again.

Each year it was the same. Sue entered the baked goods section, where she usually took first place, and Evelyn entered the jam category, where she was known as the village's star jam-maker.

Both entered the other's categories and sometimes took a placing. Neither woman minded. They discussed their methods and recipes and had no rivalry. They enjoyed the challenge and were philosophical about the outcome.

Their husbands, on the other hand, took the vegetable categories very seriously and were rivals in all sections, winning turn and turn about but hating the other's successes.

It made the women laugh but was also a source of irritation because they could never do anything as a foursome since the men wouldn't speak to each other.

If anything, however, their husbands' animosity over the years had brought the women closer.

* * * *

A week later, Sue pulled back her bedroom curtains and was pleased to find it bright and sunny.

She'd heard Tony get up at dawn. No doubt he'd headed down to the allotment to select his prized vegetables and get them washed and sorted.

Sue showered and had breakfast before calling on Evelyn.

"Shall we go and help set up?" she asked.

They spent the morning setting out tables and chairs in the tea tent and putting big tables into position in the judging marquee. Children darted in and out, excited by all the action. A bouncy castle had been set up ready for the two o'clock opening.

At one p.m. Sue wiped a layer of sweat from her brow with the back of her hand.

"Right, home for a quick shower and then I'll bring my cakes and stuff back."

"Me, too," Evelyn said. "Have you seen the men?"

"No, no sign," Sue told her.

* * * *

Sue and Evelyn spent the afternoon working in the tea tent and only stopped at four p.m., ready for the judging. They stood in the eerie light of the canvas marquee as a microphone crackled into life and the Reverend Marshall cleared his throat.

"Ladies and gentlemen, welcome to Grindling Village Show. This has been another good year for us, with much money raised for local charities including –" he coughed lightly "– the church roof."

People smiled and clapped gently.

"Now, on to the important part," he went on. "It's good to see terrific participation from everybody and I'm especially happy to see the efforts made by the youngsters."

"Does that mean Phil and Tony?" Evelyn whispered to Sue.

Sue covered her mouth as she gave a snort of laughter.

"Now, the first category is for cakes and we have a winner." The reverend paused dramatically and Evelyn gripped Sue's arm.

"Sue Richards, for her amazing chocolate brownies. Sue, would you like to come and collect your prize, and would you be willing to make some for the vicarage coffee morning?"

Sue grinned and walked forward to loud applause.

The judging went on. Evelyn got a second place for her blackberry and apple jam and third for her rhubarb and ginger.

"Now, we turn to the important job of judging the vegetable section," the reverend said.

Sue looked across the tent. She could just see Tony's face creased in a deep frown. Phil stood a few people back, also looking tense.

"The winner in the onion category is a newcomer to the village, Ron Smythe. It's nice to see some new participants this year." Sue turned to look at Evelyn, who shrugged.

"I don't know him," she whispered.

Sue looked across at Tony. His face, even in the canvas light, was a deep plum colour. He usually won the onion category.

"Next we have broad beans and the winner is . . ." the reverend paused dramatically. "Ron Smythe again."

"I don't think I want to go home this evening," Sue whispered to Evelyn.

"Me, neither. Phil will be spitting feathers. Who is this Ron Smythe?"

"No idea," Sue said.

The prize-giving continued. Phil had a first place for his carrots and Tony for tomatoes but most of the awards went to Ron.

"And finally the overall cup this year goes to . . ." The microphone crackled. "Ron Smythe."

The tent was quiet for a moment as if everybody was taking in the news, then it erupted in a tsunami of conversation and clapping.

"That's the first time in years neither Tony nor Phil has won," Evelyn said.

Sue shook her head. She turned to look for Tony and was surprised to see him step towards Phil.

"Ev, look!" Sue nodded in the direction of their husbands.

"Well, I never." Evelyn looked at Sue, her eyes wide. "It's taken someone else beating them for them to talk to each other."

"I'm very happy to say that the produce from the show today is being donated to St Thomas's hospice . . ." The reverend continued speaking but neither Sue nor Evelyn listened. They were watching as their husbands stood holding their first face-to-face conversation in many years.

*   *   *   *

A week later Sue and Evelyn were at the local National Trust house, sitting in the courtyard of the converted stables café.

"This is lovely," Sue said, stretching out in the sun.

"It's fabulous," Evelyn agreed. "Do you think we should order for the men or go ahead?"

"I think they might be a while," Sue said. "Last time I saw them, they had collared the head gardener and were quizzing him about the onions they grow. Phil was making notes and Tony was checking things on his phone."

"They're taking it seriously," Evelyn said. "They've decided to pool resources in order to beat this Ron Smythe next year."

"Do you know who he is?" Sue asked. "Or where he lives?"

Evelyn shook her head.

"No idea. But he obviously knows his onions!" ∎

Glen Lyon, Perthshire

There's little surprise why Glen Lyon was once described as the "longest, loneliest and loveliest" of glens, and it's not just Sir Walter Scott whose heart it captured, but other literary greats such as Tennyson and Wordsworth, too. At around 32 miles, this enclosed Perthshire glen is home to a wide array of wildlife, from red squirrel to deer, which thrive in a landscape where the colours change with the seasons, autumn bringing the most vibrant hues. Among the trees are birch, beech, chestnut, sycamore and Scots pine.

Rising above the south side of Glen Lyon is Ben Lawers, a majestic 3,983 feet and tenth highest in Scotland.

The beauty of Glen Lyon belies its bloody past, and with its castles and forts the area is steeped in history. Of course, this is clan country, and MacGregor's Leap is a name that remains to this day – a reminder of desperate times when Gregor MacGregor had to make this daring jump over the deep gorge in the 1560s in order to flee the Campbells, who were baying for blood. He did survive that particular close call, though his luck was soon to run out.

Possibilities

by Rosemary Gemmell

Set in the 1960s

M AM! Kirsty's away to see her boyfriend again."
Ignoring her sister's shrill cry, Kirsty hurried down the stairs two at a time and out through the close.
"Stop that yelling and come and help me with the wee one." She heard her mother's reply before the door banged shut.

Freedom! Kirsty slowed down as she passed the last few straggling post-war prefabs and dull, grey tenements on the incline. Almost there.

The heather-clad hills welcomed her at last and she breathed in the fresh air.

It was cold for August, even in Scotland, though heat began to prickle her skin after the fast walk.

Unzipping her red anorak, she pulled off the cream beret, shook her long dark hair free and twirled around with joy. Laughing and dizzy, she sank on to the heather to catch her breath, before heading to her special place.

She sometimes felt guilty at leaving Sheena behind, but not because she was meeting any boy.

"Can I no' go with you?" her sister always pleaded whenever Kirsty made her escape.

"No, Sheena, I need to be on my own sometimes."

It was true. She had to escape the confined tenement flat and responsibility for the wee ones whenever she got the chance; to have time to think and dream and read.

Her favourite flat, oval rock sat in the middle of a small forest of fir trees.

She had found it by accident one day and liked to sit imagining all the things she'd do with her life in a few years' time, when she could eventually escape the small town and narrow existence.

She'd heard the new decade called the Swinging Sixties but had no idea who was swinging what or where.

With four of them crammed into the small two-bedroomed flat along with their mother and stepfather, Kirsty often wished for her own space.

Because she was fifteen, Mam expected her to look after the younger

ones, and though Sheena was eleven, there was still five-year-old Sam and toddler Rosie.

Money hardly stretched among them all, though rationing had come to an end some years ago, after the terrible long war.

At least her stepdad worked extra hours at the shipyards to make some overtime, and Mam did her best at spreading out the housekeeping.

Kirsty sometimes liked to help her make the big pots of lentil and vegetable soup that kept them healthy and stomachs full, especially when she got to eat the last piece of raw carrot so her mum wouldn't grate her fingers.

But she did not like the thick, creamy-coloured tripe that she had to chew for ever. It never seemed to boil tender enough, though the milky potatoes and onions were tasty enough.

Her favourite treat was the boiled beef Mam ordered from the butcher when they had enough money – sliced deliciousness served with roast potatoes, carrots and salty gravy.

But Kirsty was almost sure another bairn was on the way. Mam's stomach was getting bigger, though she'd never tell Kirsty anything until she had to.

She'd only warned her about becoming a woman in time, when Kirsty turned thirteen and worried about the changes happening to her body.

They'd talked about it in the playground at school, but none of the girls knew much more than she did.

She hated the idea of another brother or sister to look after. Hugging her knees, she dreamed again of living in a huge house like those in Eldon Place with their long drives edged with pretty plants and wee white chucky stones.

She would travel to all the countries studied in Geography and read all the story books in the world, without being constantly interrupted whenever she wanted some peace.

She still hadn't managed to finish "Jane Eyre". She'd been working her way through the classics and Mr Rochester had really grabbed her imagination; maybe she'd meet someone like him one day.

She resented having to leave school as soon as she was old enough to help in the house and to look for paid work. She loved learning and often read to the younger children.

Since getting enough books was a problem, she haunted the library and had long given up trying to explain to her friends why she had to visit it so much.

They were only interested in the latest fashion and the new hot pop stars. This year Elvis Presley and Cliff Richard vied for their adoration. She couldn't see the fuss herself.

A sudden noise told Kirsty she was no longer alone. She jumped to her feet.

One of the most beautiful dogs she'd ever seen padded into view, tongue lolling, its face almost smiling as it panted up to her.

"Hello, boy." She stroked the shaggy golden hair.

The dog heard the other sound before she did. Kirsty looked up in surprise, as two figures came into the clearing.

"There you are."

A middle-aged woman walked towards her, eyes on the dog.

Then Kirsty noticed the second figure. A girl, about fourteen maybe, with beautiful long fair hair and a pretty face like a princess in the old fairy-tale books.

"I hope Bracken didn't upset you." The woman smiled at Kirsty.

"Oh, is that his name? No, he's lovely. I love animals."

Kirsty looked at the girl. She hadn't moved at all and seemed to be staring.

"We often come up here." The woman turned to the girl and, taking her arm, brought her over to Kirsty. "This is Lily, my daughter. What's your name, child?"

Kirsty was speechless for a moment. The girl was blind! Then she realised she was staring.

"My name is Kirsty."

"I used to love coming up here." Lily suddenly spoke in a soft voice.

"After I had my accident, it was one of the things I missed most.

"But I can still smell the pine and the grass and feel the springiness of the heather, and I love the sound of lambs bleating, don't you?"

Kirsty thought Lily had the sweetest voice and was amazed at the matter of fact way she seemed to accept not being able to see all of this. Yet she'd described exactly the same things Kirsty liked.

As they strolled along the path, she discovered Lily loved the countryside and books as much as she did.

"I can't read them myself now, of course," Lily said. "But Mother is good at reading to me when she has time."

Kirsty was struck again at how accepting the girl seemed. She couldn't imagine not being able to see the glorious words that made up a story.

And no-one would ever read to her, so she'd be completely lost in her own dull world. How horrible!

Lily paused to stroke her dog.

"Why don't you come and visit me one day next week? We live in Eldon Place."

Kirsty could hear the note of hope in the girl's voice. She swallowed her nerves at hearing where they lived and answered brightly.

"That'd be great. If that's OK?" She turned to Lily's mother, not sure if she'd feel the same.

"Please do come, my dear. Lily needs some young company and Bracken obviously likes you."

An idea popped into Kirsty's head as she spoke.

"Maybe I could read to you, Lily. I'm good at it and I love books."

"That's an excellent idea, Kirsty. I'm sure Lily would much rather have someone nearer her own age to read to her, and you could discuss the stories afterwards."

"Oh, Kirsty, I'd love you to read to me. But can you spare the time?" Lily asked.

Kirsty thought quickly. It might be difficult some days, and she'd have to give up some of her walks in the hills, unless Lily came with her. But she'd make the time.

If Lily loved books so much, then they'd probably have plenty to read, and she wasn't going to miss that chance. Anyway, she liked the girl and wanted to see her again.

"I'll sort it out with Mam. Do you want me to come the day after tomorrow for an hour? See how we get on?"

"Excellent, Kirsty. I'll write down our address and we'll expect you about two o'clock. I'm Mrs Harrison."

Kirsty shook the hand the woman held out to her and was warmed by her friendly smile.

She waved goodbye with a lighter heart. She'd found a new friend and maybe the chance to spend some time with that lovely dog.

And imagine being asked to read to someone. She'd enjoy doing different voices to bring the characters alive. What could be better?

So what if she lived in the crush of a small flat with a noisy family? She'd have some time away and maybe, if there was a new bairn, they'd get a bigger house one day and could have a dog of their own for the younger ones.

Meantime, she was lucky enough when she compared herself to Lily's life without sight.

As she got nearer home, Kirsty came down to earth. Instinctively, she knew her stepdad wouldn't be too happy. He already teased her about "high-falutin' ideas" just because she liked to read and had dreams that stretched beyond the street they lived in.

She hadn't really liked him at first when he started coming round to see Mam.

When her own dad died a few years after Sheena's birth, Kirsty recognised her mam's deep sadness. She'd pushed her own grief aside so she could help with Sheena, but she missed her gentle dad with his silly jokes.

Kirsty hadn't understood exactly but knew the man she called Uncle Tommy was a threat to the life she and Sheena had with their mam.

She tried to be nice to him, but didn't like his burliness, or the coarse way he spoke sometimes. Yet her mother smiled more often and he worked hard.

She'd gradually realised it was just his way and he was always kind to them. She wanted Mam to be happy, so when they got married, she kept quiet and escaped into her books or out to the countryside.

Now, as she returned home, Kirsty's elation seeped away like the air from a burst balloon.

She didn't want to keep secrets from her family but was determined to see Lily and Bracken again – not to mention all the books inside a house in Eldon Place!

She began to drop hints next evening, about meeting a girl and her dog in the hills and being invited to her house.

"That's nice, pet," her mother said, distracted by serving the meal. "Where did you say she lives?"

Kirsty swallowed and glanced at her stepdad, but he seemed preoccupied with his food.

"Eldon Place," she answered quietly. "Lily's blind and she'd like me to go and visit her."

"Oh, so the people here are no' good enough for ye these days, eh? Eldon Place? That wid suit ye right fine, wi' yer high ideas."

Kirsty ignored the taunts as she always did, though she caught his grin and a wink to show he didn't really mean it. But she was glad when her mam replied.

"Stop teasing the lass, Tommy. You go and enjoy yourself for a change, Kirsty. You're a great help to me, but Sheena is good with the two wee ones now and can take a turn now and then."

Kirsty smiled at the thought of a whole new life beckoning. She might never live in a house in Eldon Place, but she was determined to learn from the people there, and from all the stories she had yet to read.

She'd be a true friend to Lily, so the blind girl could see everything through her words.

And together they would explore the worlds of imagination, of dreams and possibilities. ■

Vintage Cleaning Tips
from the "Friend"

Lemons

LEMON trees are very pretty – and the fruit is pretty useful, too. Citrus fruits aren't just refreshingly tasty; their acidic juice can make short work of tasks around the home, with no toxic residues. In fact, limonene, one of the natural compounds in the oil of citrus fruit peels, is used by industry in the manufacture of solvents and fragrance ingredients for cosmetic and cleaning products.

You could just go back to the source, though, and use the fruit directly.

Ink-bottle accidents in 1957 needed a quick response to rescue the unlucky carpet or garment. "When the stain is still wet," the "Friend" wrote, "cover it thickly with salt. Scrape up the salt with a spoon, applying fresh salt until no more ink is absorbed. Then rub the spot with a cut lemon and rinse with fresh water."

Remember lighting the stove with matches? It happened a lot in 1902, and walls suffered. Nevertheless, a handy lemon could come to the rescue.

"Marks on the kitchen walls, which have been made by careless hands in striking matches, will disappear if rubbed with the cut surface of a lemon, then with a cloth dipped in whitening. Wash the surface with warm soap and water, and quickly wipe with a clean cloth wrung from clear water."

Wandering into the 1961 kitchen – what's that strange whiff? Ah, it's the cutlery we used on Friday. Clean, but with a lingering aroma. The "Friend" knew what to do, though! "To remove the "fishy" smell from fish forks and knives, give them a rub with a piece of lemon after they have been washed," readers were advised.

For help with stains, marks and nasty niffs – a lemon is your friend! ▪

Shutterstock.

On The Mend

by Teresa Ashby

N O!" Rosie cried when she saw the trellis had been beaten down by the wind, dragging the glorious honeysuckle with it. She raced outside into the howling wind and rain and tried to push it back up, but it was futile. The struts had snapped and the trellis looked beyond repair.

There had to be some way to save it! Dan had built it from scratch.

Everything in the garden had been made by Dan, from the trellis to the table and benches.

He'd crafted it all with love and care and, even as he worked, he'd known he wouldn't be around much longer.

"I'm leaving things behind that will make your life better," he'd said when she begged him not to work so hard.

She knelt down on the sodden ground and began to snip at the honeysuckle.

The trellis was the only thing left that hadn't succumbed to the wind over the years in one way or another.

"Rosie? You out here?"

She turned to see Thomo coming in through the side gate – the gate that Dan had made and Thomo had repaired three years ago after the wind had blown it right off its hinges.

Thomo was Dan's best friend, and he'd been checking in on Rosie regularly since Dan died five years ago.

"When did this happen?" he asked.

"Just now! That wind!"

"You're soaked," Thomo remarked, his face creasing with concern.

Rosie noticed how the rain clung to his eyelashes before dripping down his face, and how unbothered he seemed, but that was Thomo all over.

"Why don't you go in and put the kettle on and I'll see what I can do," he suggested.

Illustration by Manon Gandiolle.

She looked up into his kind blue eyes and nodded as he helped her to her feet.

His blond hair had already turned dark in the rain, but he seemed oblivious.

Whenever she needed help he materialised as if by magic. He knew how the wind made her edgy and how upset she got when Dan's things were damaged.

While she waited for the kettle to boil, she watched Thomo working.

He was cutting the honeysuckle away from the trellis, salvaging as much as he could of the plant.

The trellis was in bits, and at one point he held a piece of shattered wood in his hand and seemed to stare despairingly at it.

"Coffee's ready," she called, and he dropped the piece of wood he was holding and hurried inside.

"Do you think you can fix it, Thomo?" Rosie asked.

"Of course I can," Thomo replied without a moment's hesitation.

"I can't thank you enough," she began.

"You don't have to thank me," he said. "I promised Dan I'd keep an eye on you, so I'm just keeping my word."

"Well, you don't have to," Rosie replied. "It's been five years and you have your own life to live."

Thomo shrugged.

"Which you're a part of, like it or not," he replied. "We're family. I'll pop out to get some bits to repair the trellis."

"But it's Saturday," Rosie reminded him. "Surely you have plans."

"No plans." He drained his coffee mug. "I'll be back in a bit."

While Thomo was gone, Rosie looked out at the garden.

The bird table Dan made was knocked over by the wind the year after he died. Rosie thought her heart would break as she'd picked up the pieces, watched by hungry birds.

Thomo had found her in floods of tears and offered to go out and get a replacement, but that had made her cry even harder.

"Dan made it for me," she explained. "I can't throw it away."

So Thomo had put it back together and it was as good as new.

It had been the same with the gate. Thomo had offered to get a metal one to replace it, but she got so upset at the idea that he went to get some wood, new hinges and a handle instead.

Then there was the table. The wind hadn't just blown it over, it had rolled it across the garden and smashed it into the wall.

"We can get another table," Thomo suggested, but she didn't want another one. She wanted Dan's.

So more wood was bought and Thomo rebuilt it.

By the time the pergola fell down, Thomo had fixed it without even suggesting a replacement.

"Go into town, meet up with a friend and have a coffee," he said every time. "It'll all be done when you get back."

While Thomo was fetching the wood, the rain stopped and the sun broke through the clouds, making the grass and leaves twinkle.

Rosie looked at the remains of the trellis now that most of the honeysuckle had been cut away.

There was precious little left of it and not a single piece of wood was complete.

"What are you going to do this afternoon?" Thomo asked Rosie when he returned.

"I thought I might help you," she replied, and his eyebrows rose.

"I don't need any help. You should go into town, meet up with a friend and have a coffee. It's lovely now and the wind's dropped."

It was his usual spiel.

"All right," Rosie agreed. "If you're sure."

He looked relieved. He always worked super-fast.

Did he have someone else come round to help him? If so, she'd like to know who it was so she could thank them, too.

She drove round the corner, then walked back home.

She could hear Thomo's merry whistling as she walked up the front path.

Upstairs, she watched him as he worked, hidden by the net curtain.

When Thomo had made the new trellis, he took off the broken struts

The Coffee Shop

From my table in the window, I watch the world go by . . .
It's great to take a moment, before I have to fly.
The clouds are hanging heavy, but they don't dent my mood
When I'm sipping on a latte and savouring my food.

The aroma of fresh coffee, the hiss of the machine,
The hum of conversation, my favourite magazine.
Ah, how I love to sit here, it gives me such a lift —
Best get behind the counter now, it's time to start my shift!

Marian Cleworth

and put up new ones. The new ones were much sturdier than the old ones.

Then he sorted through the broken bits and carefully placed one piece on the new trellis before attaching it to the wall.

It made her look again at the bird table. What on that was original?

She'd noticed before how part of the roof was a slightly different colour to the rest, but had never thought anything of it. The stand was much chunkier than Dan's original.

Same with the table. One plank was a different colour from the rest and the legs were much heavier.

As for the gate, now she thought about it, the only part of it that was original was the bolt!

The new hinges Thomo had fixed to it were bigger and stronger than Dan's.

When he'd finished putting the trellis up, Thomo carefully wound some of the longer strands of honeysuckle through it and Rosie slipped out to fetch her car.

He was washing his hands when she got back.

"Did you have a good afternoon?" Thomo asked her.

"Very good," she replied. "I had a bit of an epiphany today."

"What was that?"

"I'll tell you later. Show me what you've done."

Rosie stood in front of the wall and saw the small piece of Dan's trellis there amongst all the new wood.

"Dan's trellis, as good as new," he declared.

"Like the gate." Rosie nodded. "And the bird table, and all the other bits and pieces you've repaired over the years."

Thomo smiled.

"I hope Dan would be pleased," he said. "He taught me everything I know about woodwork."

"I think he'd be over the moon," she replied. "But you must have noticed there was a flaw in all of Dan's projects."

"Was there?" Thomo asked, looking startled.

"You know very well there was. He didn't build things to last. He built them to break, knowing that you would come to the rescue."

Thomo looked puzzled. He scratched his head and a piece of honeysuckle fell out of his hair.

Rosie plucked another piece from beside his ear.

"You really think that's what he did?" he asked.

"I realised today," she admitted. "And when things broke that couldn't be fixed, you made something new, but every time you salvaged a little piece of the original so that it would still be Dan's."

Thomo looked mortified.

"I'm sorry, Rosie. I didn't mean to deceive you. I never understood why Dan had left weaknesses in everything. It never made sense."

"You didn't deceive me, Thomo." Rosie smiled. "The stuff you made is new, but you saved a little bit of Dan so the memories are intact."

Thomo let out a sigh of relief.

"I thought you'd be upset," he admitted.

"You could have given up on me a long time ago," Rosie murmured. "Why didn't you?"

He'd never been able to lie to her.

She held her breath, waiting for his answer.

"Because I love you, Rosie," Thomo said brokenly. "I'm sorry."

"Why are you sorry? My heart will always have a piece of Dan in there, but the repair is strong." Rosie smiled. "That's your work, Thomo."

"Mine?" He looked up, his eyes full of hope.

She reached for his hand, which was covered in scratches.

He squeezed her fingers gently.

"I love you, too, Thomo," Rosie said.

And when they kissed, the wind dropped and seemed to sigh happily, as if Dan had been the wind, creating havoc, but knowing that Thomo would restore order – not just to the garden, but to Rosie's life.

Perhaps that had been his plan all along. ∎

Illustration by Gerard Fay.

Waste Not, Want Not

by Maggie Cobbett

I CAN'T remember the last time I tasted chocolate," Trevor grumbled. "It's been ages since we won the war and I thought that everything would be much better by now."

His mother sighed and put down the jersey that she was darning for the umpteenth time. At least darning wool wasn't rationed, although the choice of colours was very limited

"Over a year, yes, lad. But nobody ever really wins wars. They just bring grief and suffering all round.

"Anyway, we'd be hard pressed to afford chocolate even if sweet rationing had stopped. What with your dad still away and the doctor's bill owing . . .

"Maybe I should have put our Maisie into a nursery after all and registered for war work, but I just didn't like to leave her with anyone else."

Mrs Gower glanced over to the well-worn clippy rug by the cold hearth, where the youngest member of the family was playing listlessly with a battered teddy bear.

Born weeks before she should have been, Maisie had failed to thrive as a baby and still looked undernourished.

The loving care the whole family bestowed on her in abundance was simply not enough.

Trevor flushed, his freckled face full of concern.

"I'm sorry, Mum," he muttered. "Of course you shouldn't have done that. That's not what I meant at all. It's just that . . ."

A thin hand reached up to pat his cheek.

At twelve, he was really shooting up and his mother noted sadly that the sleeves of his latest shirt, obtained from the WVS clothing exchange, barely skimmed his wrists.

His well scuffed shoes, on the other hand, were a size too large, but at least he'd soon grow into them.

"I know, son," she said, "and it's not all bad, you know. I expect we'll pull through one way or another.

"At least it's warm enough for us to do without a fire and that's a big saving."

"We're nearly out of coal, anyway. There are only a few more shovels' worth left in the cellar."

Trevor flexed his skinny arm, thinking of all the times during the winter that he'd filled the coal scuttle and lugged it back up to the kitchen.

He dimly remembered his father doing the same before he left for the war, saying that it wasn't woman's work.

It had become so, though, before Trevor grew strong enough to carry the heavy iron scuttle.

He'd dropped it the first time and scattered coal all over the cellar steps. His big sister had wiped away his tears of humiliation and helped him to pick it all up.

Fourteen-year-old Rose looked up from her own sewing and smiled. Clever with her hands, she was busily transforming an almost completely worn-out felt hat into something fit to put on for church.

"The last time I had chocolate was when the GIs drove through town on their way to the American air base," she said. "Do you remember? They were going home and one of them threw me a Hershey bar. It wasn't a patch on Cadbury's, was it?"

"How would I know?" Trevor grumbled, no longer contrite. "You didn't share it with me, although you did give Maisie a piece and she got it all over her face."

Rose frowned.

"Well, you didn't share the gum you caught, either. Not that Mum would have let Maisie have any of that in case she swallowed it."

"No," he admitted. "I didn't, but I didn't chew it, either. I swapped it with Ernie Barraclough for a piece of shrapnel he'd found.

"It's not an enemy one, worse luck, but it's the best in my collection so far.

"Ernie's is better, because he's out there looking every day. He's even got the nose cone of an anti-aircraft shell with two fuse band rings still attached and –"

"I don't care what he's got," Rose snapped. "What if he finds something that hasn't exploded?

"Only a boy would be stupid enough to go poking around on a bomb site after all the warnings we've had."

"And only a girl would sit around the house all day sewing a stupid old hat!" he retaliated.

"Now, now, that's quite enough from you two!" Mrs Gower chided. "Chocolate's bad for your teeth, anyway, and I've never been able to see the point of chewing-gum.

"As for shrapnel collections of all things, you must promise me, Trevor, that you won't go anywhere near those bomb sites. I want you in one piece when your father comes home.

"All the same, I wish we did have something that we could swap or sell right now.

"The district nurse said that Maisie needs even more milk and eggs than the priority scheme allows. That's the only way that she's going to build up her strength."

"You wouldn't use the Black Market, Mum?" Rose was shocked.

"No. Of course not. Even if I could afford it, which I can't. We've got enough ration points between us, but finding the money to pay for anything extra is quite another thing."

Getting by on the small allowance allotted to the family of a serving soldier had always been a struggle and yet Mrs Gower generally managed to put on a brave face.

Now, though, she was struggling to hide her despair as she looked round the sparsely furnished room. The older children, their quarrel forgotten, gazed at her in dismay.

"Your dad made good money before the war," she continued quietly, "and will again when he comes back. But I don't know how much longer we can carry on like this."

"Surely he'll be home soon," Trevor said. "Ernie's father was demobbed ages ago, and his big brothers, too, even the one who was a Bevin Boy. They're all back at work."

"I know, but there are plenty of other men still waiting their turn and it could be quite a while yet."

"And will Dad's old job at the factory still be there for him?"

"So he was promised and I don't think Baines and Co. can go back on that."

"They won't," Rose assured her. "Susan Baines is in my Sunday school

Wonderland

Brown and russet, red and gold,
A magical display,
Now telling us that summer
Has really slipped away.
A cooler breeze is whispering
And stirring all the trees,
As fleecy clouds go travelling
To taunt us and to tease.

The river flowing gently on,
Now peaceful and serene,
Forgets the springtime storms and gales
When many floods were seen.
The purple hills are looking down,
Protecting, strong and kind,
So let this autumn wonderland
Uplift your heart and mind.

Iris Hesselden.

class and she's told everyone that her father never breaks his word.

"He said that the women who've been working for him during the war have done a great job, but he only ever saw it as a temporary arrangement.

"I'm not sure that's quite fair, though. Some of them might want to stay on."

"Well, love, life isn't fair," Mrs Gower reminded her. "It never has been and it never will be."

Rose nodded.

"So we'll just have to keep our chins up and do whatever it takes until things get better. Isn't that what you've always said, Mum?"

Mrs Gower collected herself and dabbed her eyes with a corner of her shabby pinafore.

"Of course we must, Rose. We're all safe and sound. your father, too, and we've still got a home for him to come back to. That's what counts, after all."

A smile illuminated her careworn face as she knelt down to scoop little Maisie into her arms.

It could have been a great deal worse, she thought to herself.

The bombs that had rained down on Hull had missed their street, although not by much, and Maisie at least would soon forget the screech of the sirens and what it was like to cower in the cellar night after night.

Many families were less fortunate, their former homes reduced to rubble or with a whole side blown away, leaving them looking like giant doll's-houses.

Marauding children loved to make dens in the unstable ruins and quite a few had come to grief when floorboards had collapsed without warning.

"Well, that's done," Rose announced, snapping off her thread and holding up the hat for inspection. "What do you think, Mum?"

"Lovely, my dear. I'd never have recognised it."

Mrs Gower had taught her daughter the basics of sewing and knitting while she was still at junior school but freely admitted that Rose had long outstripped her when it came to creativity.

The formerly plain hat, so faded that its original colour could only be guessed at, now sported a carefully embroidered brim and a posy of flowers created from tiny scraps of fabric.

"Not bad," Trevor said, which was, from him, a compliment of the highest order.

*   *   *   *

Rose's cheeks were pink with excitement when she and Trevor came out of Sunday school and found their mother and little sister waiting to walk home with them.

"You'll never guess what, Mum," she said. "The other girls thought my hat was lovely and wanted to know where it came from."

"Did you tell them that your auntie Hilda was planning to give it to a jumble sale?"

"Of course I didn't. They couldn't see where the flowers I embroidered covered the really thin parts. I'm so glad that you kept all those tiny bits of wool."

"Well, I nearly didn't. There'd have been more knots than stitches if I'd tried to knit anything with them.

"Even make do and mend has its limits and I've certainly done my share of that over the last few years."

Rose smiled, remembering all the outgrown garments that her mother had painstakingly unpicked in order to reuse the wool.

They had wound it round the back of a chair and washed it to take out the curl, but that couldn't prevent each new creation being a bit nobbly.

"Those bits are perfect for me, though, Mum," she said. "Susan Baines has asked me to go round to her house and see if I can do something with one of her hats.

"She's used all her own clothing coupons and wants a new one for her cousin's wedding, but her father says no.

"May I, Mum? Susan's promised to pay me half a crown if I make a good job of it, and she'll recommend me to her friends as well."

Mrs Gower considered.

"All right, I suppose so, as long as it doesn't interfere with your homework."

"Oh, Mum, it will help Maisie, and I'll be old enough to leave in a few months' time anyway."

"Which doesn't necessarily mean that you will. Dad and I have always been keen for you to make something of yourself.

"Now don't pull that face, Rose. We'll just have to wait and see, won't we?"

*   *   *   *

Susan Baines was delighted when she saw the brightly coloured flowers and birds that had appeared on her previously serviceable but very plain hat.

She was as good as her word, too, and soon Rose was working on half a dozen commissions.

Styles varied from a simple beret to a "pudding basin", its brim previously beaten into shape in an attempt to make it look more fashionable.

A turban, a fedora, a cocktail hat with a veil and a cloche someone's aunt had worn in the 1920s were added to the mix, all to be brightened up for reuse.

Rose's hats became the talk of the neighbourhood and every penny she earned benefited the family. It wasn't a fortune, but it certainly helped and she loved doing it.

If only there was more money in it, Rose thought, she would have happily spent her life remodelling hats for her friends.

*   *   *   *

Her efforts were unexpectedly rewarded when word reached the ear of the headmaster, who asked to speak to Rose and her mother one day after school.

"My wife tells me that she's never seen anything prettier than those hats," he began, "and talent like that shouldn't be wasted in a humdrum job.

"Have you ever thought of apprenticing Rose to a milliner, Mrs Gower? I have someone in mind who'd be more than happy to take her on."

"It's a good idea," she replied, shifting Maisie to a more comfortable position on her lap, "but first I'll have to see what her father has to say about it."

Her face broke into a happy smile.

"This arrived just before we left home, you see, and he's going to be so proud of her."

She was clutching a telegram and the joy on her face left no-one in any doubt that it contained good news. ■

Vintage Cleaning Tips from the "Friend"

From The Larder

EVERYDAY foodstuffs came in handy for many chores. In 1902, readers could send pesky moths packing with help from their spice jars.

"Whole cloves are used to exterminate the moth," the "Friend" informed them. "It is said that they are more effectual as a destroying agent than either tobacco, camphor or cedar-shavings."

In 1961, laundry woes were solved with ingenious use of fruit and vegetables. Found rust marks on the material? Simply "chop up some rhubarb and boil in a little water until reduced by half. Using this solution, boil the stained article for quarter of an hour."

Perhaps an incident with the iron had left a scorch mark. No need for tears. "Rub scorched linen with a piece of raw onion, and leave for a short time. Then soak in cold water and the scorch mark will fade."

A surprising use for potatoes was shared in 1882.

"Before dipping a new pen into ink," the "Friend" advised, "thrust it into a fresh cut potato, and the ink will never cling. When the pen is thickly gummed with dried ink a few thrusts will clean it perfectly. When not in use, some accountants leave their pens sticking into a potato kept on the desk for the purpose." Fancy that!

One of the most useful cleaning tips appeared in 1894.

"The old-fashioned way of cleaning wallpaper is perhaps the simplest and best," the writer said. "After carefully removing all the dust, cut a piece of bread from a stale loaf, free from crust. Begin at the top of the room and wipe lightly downward, about half a yard at each stroke, and thus continue till all the paper has been gone over. Some papers will only stand to be rubbed very lightly, and the surface of the bread should be renewed from time to time."

In 2021 English Heritage tested historic home cleaning methods and found that "white bread [. . .] can collect an impressive amount of dirt when used on wallpaper."

Shutterstock.

A Thousand Words

—— by Tess Niland Kimber ——

ENRI DUBOIS smiled. It had taken 40 years, but he was now being declared "an overnight success" by the top art critics. He stood quietly in a corner of the London gallery, dressed in a long dark coat and wide-brimmed hat that covered his grey hair. Only his orange scarf added a flash of colour to his outfit.

He watched the visitors studying his work, proud to have an exhibition of his life's work here.

"Henri, good to see you," Jacob Franklin, the gallery's curator, greeted him. "These are the best ticket sales for years. Everyone wants to see the Dubois Portrait Exhibition. I wish we could extend it."

"I am sorry, but tomorrow we must move on. My agent – he's keen for my work to travel."

Once he would have longed for an extension, but he could not wait. Tomorrow the tour went to Bournemouth. Nothing must delay him.

"No problem. We'll re-book later in the year."

Henri smiled at Jacob. In the old days, in France, he'd arranged his own shows. They'd been modest affairs – for rural village halls, small art galleries, maybe local town halls.

Then the film "Girl With The Pearl Earring" had revived interest in portraiture and his career had benefited.

Even at his large studio at home in Brittany he only had space to hang some of his work on the walls. It was wonderful to see all his paintings together.

Works such as Felicity, Marie et Nicole, Suzanne and his most famous portrait of all, Louise . . .

*   *   *   *

Young Henri's Dubois' studio off Park Road in Bournemouth was filled with light. Music poured from his transistor radio as he painted.

Frantically Henri covered the large canvas with a mix of oils from his

Illustration by Shutterstock.

palette. Paint splattered his arms and smock. He must finish before his next class at the art college this afternoon.

Suddenly there was a knock on his door. Cursing the interruption, he set down his palette and brush.

Opening the door, he felt his breath being sucked from his body.

Before him stood the most beautiful girl wearing a checked cheesecloth shirt and a pair of flared jeans.

Dainty, blonde with elfin features, she reminded him of a cross between Brigitte Bardot and Leslie Caron.

"*Bonjour,*" he said, then, remembering where he was, he corrected himself. "Hello."

"Hello," the young girl said tentatively. "I've come about the job."

His English was not good, and he took a few moments to work out what she'd said.

"Job?" he repeated.

"You are Henry Dubois?"

"Henri," he corrected. "I am French. And you are . . .?"

"Louise Carpenter." She held out her hand. "You advertised in the newsagent's for a model to sit for a portrait."

Henri could not believe his luck. He would love to paint this beautiful girl.

"Come in," he said, beckoning her into the small studio. "Sorry – the mess."

"Do you like the Kinks, too?" she said as the song on the radio faded, carefully stepping in her platform shoes over a splodge of wet paint by his easel.

"Kinks?"

She pointed to the radio.

"Ah, yes, I do. Sorry – my English is poor."

"Better than my French." She laughed.

Henri was so mesmerised by her light blue eyes, the tilt of her nose, the paleness of her skin, that he could hardly speak.

"So, the job?" she prompted.

"Ah, yes." He recovered. "I need a girl to sit for me. Not move. Many hours. I pay. It is for my art degree."

"Oh, you're clever." She smiled. "And you'll only paint my face?"

"Yes. I am a portrait artist. Or rather, I want to be."

The girl nodded.

"Will my face do?"

"Do?" Henri frowned.

"Is my face good enough for you to paint?" She turned her head slowly from left to right so he could examine her.

Henri smiled.

"You are . . . *parfait*."

That winter Henri spent many happy hours painting Louise. He found her fascinating.

Not only did she have the most beautiful face that was a challenge to pay justice to on the canvas, but it was the look in her eyes sometimes, when she daydreamed, that mesmerised him.

What was she thinking? He wanted to capture those thoughts, her emotions, in the portrait. Was she sad? Or just concentrating?

Unfortunately, with the work he did, they could not talk much. She had to stay perfectly still so he could replicate her beautiful features in his painting.

How he longed to ask her about her interests, her life outside the hours she spent with him in the studio but there was little opportunity.

One day, at the end of an arduous session, he plucked up the courage to ask, "Would you like to go for coffee?"

"Oh, yes, please – we could go to Marmaduke's on the seafront. Have you been?"

"I have not travelled much in Bournemouth."

"Then I'll take you." Louise smiled. "It's lovely. You can sit by the window and watch the sea, the birds flying by, the visitors on the pier."

Henri collected his long black coat and wide-brimmed hat from the peg beside the door then tied a long woollen scarf around his neck.

As they walked, they chatted about his life in France, Louise's parents and younger brother and how she hoped to find a job looking after children.

"I want to be a nanny with a good family who'll take me travelling. I want to see the world," she said.

"You must come to France," he said, feeling his cheeks redden – how bold he must sound.

"Oh, I'd love to see Paris – the Eiffel Tower, Notre Dame!"

"And, of course, le Louvre for the art."

She linked her arm through his as they walked down the steep hill to the seafront. The wind, gusting off the sea, buffeted them and she laughed when his hat almost lifted from his head.

Pushing open the door to the cosy café, they were greeted by the sounds of the Bay City Rollers singing "Bye Bye Baby" from a jukebox in the corner. Couples huddled around tables covered in red and white checked cloths.

It was very different from the Parisian cafés he used but there was a warm atmosphere he liked. But then, he thought, gazing at Louise, he'd like anywhere if he was with her.

He bought two cups of hot chocolate and they sat by a window overlooking the sea. Waves rushed on to the sand where a boy and his father were flying a yellow kite.

Henri had never been so happy. He loved being with Louise. These weeks had been such a special time for him. He was more than a little in love with her and yet felt too shy to ask her to go out with him.

Maybe this afternoon he'd find the courage.

"I love Marmaduke's," she said, sipping her drink. "But Phil prefers the pub. He always wants to go for a pint, whereas I'm happy sitting and watching the world go by over a coffee."

"Phil?" Henri asked, still smiling.

"My boyfriend."

Henri felt like the kite flying on the wind. Louise had a boyfriend! Of course, she was so beautiful, why had he imagined for a moment that she was single?

"Oh, I see. What . . . um . . . does Phil do?"

"He's a car mechanic. Hopes to have his own garage one day." Louise chatted about her boyfriend, unaware Henri was dying inside.

*   *   *   *

After that afternoon in Marmaduke's, Henri found it hard to paint Louise. He was in love with her but what could he do? She had a boyfriend.

One day when she sat for him, he was worried. She had such a pained look in her eyes. He tried to capture her expression on the canvas but couldn't without knowing what was wrong.

"Are you all right?" he asked. "You . . . do not seem yourself."

"Not really." She sighed. "I argued with Phil last night. He's always in the pub. It worries me."

Henri did not know what to say. If only he could tell her she was worth too much to be with someone who made her sad. If he was brave, he'd tell her how much he loved her and ask her to be with him.

But Henri was not brave. He could not say these words. Besides, his art course was ending. Soon he'd have to return to Paris.

Was it fair to tell her how he felt when he was leaving?

Instead, he said, "Have you told him you do not like the pub?"

"Yes." She shrugged. "But he thinks I'm nagging and then drinks even more."

*   *   *   *

It was a sad day when Henri finished his portrait of Louise. Normally he felt elated when he completed a painting but, although delighted with the work, he felt only sorrow, knowing his time with Louise was ending.

"Please come and see me if you are in town," he said.

"'Course – although I might be busy. I've a job interview next week."

"With another artist?"

"No," she said, "with a family. They need a nanny for their two children."

"You might travel, after all."

"Yes, although Phil won't like it."

"You must do what you feel you should," he offered tentatively. "The world is changing. Women are having their own careers. Their own lives."

"Perhaps." She smiled. "But not in Bournemouth."

And he sighed as he watched her leave the small studio.

✳ ✳ ✳ ✳

Now, as Henri travelled to Bournemouth on the train with his agent for the next leg of his art exhibition, he again thought of Louise.

In all these years, he'd never forgotten her. How could he? He had the painting to remember her by.

Louise had been his greatest work. The painting helped him not only gain his degree but had also launched his career.

Although his work had been slow to catch on, once it did, everyone praised his portrait of the enigmatic Louise.

He had much to thank her for and had tried to find her many times, but how could he? He only knew her name and that she lived in Bournemouth.

For years, he concentrated on his career, although he often thought of Louise. Eventually, he met another woman. Marie owned the art shop where he bought his paints.

They married and for 30 years lived happily in a converted stone barn, where he had a large studio. It was there that they brought up their son Pierre and daughter Giselle.

Sadly, three years ago, he'd lost Marie, and it was only his painting that had kept him sane.

When his work began to sell, no matter how much he was offered, he refused to part with his portrait of Louise.

"Why do you not sell that painting, Papa? You have been offered so much money for it," Giselle asked.

He'd told her then about the young girl he'd met in Bournemouth all those years ago and how much she'd meant to him.

"But you did not keep in touch?"

"It was not so easy. She did not even have a telephone at her home."

His daughter studied him with dark eyes.

"Why not find her now? You could look online."

"I am no good with the internet – you know that."

"No." She laughed, looking so like her mother. "But I am. Let me try to find her."

At first Henri was reluctant.

"She must have her own family. She won't remember me."

"A famous artist whose top portrait is of her face? I am sure she will remember, Papa."

Henri had shrugged it off. By that evening, he'd forgotten Giselle's promise until a few days later when she visited again.

"I think I have found your Louise on Facebook."

"She's not my Louise." He'd smiled, trying to hide his excitement.

Giselle tapped on her phone while Henri reached for his reading glasses.

"Is this Louise?"

Henri studied the smiling photo of a woman with a cloud of white hair and a beaming smile.

"I do not think . . ." But then he looked closer.

Was it her? He knew her features so well but it was difficult to tell. Obviously, she was older – he'd last seen her in the mid-1970s – but it wasn't that.

"It might be."

"Look at these other photos." Giselle showed him several other pictures – some taken when she was younger.

"Yes, that is my. . . I mean, Louise." He smiled.

"Why not send her a message? Ask if she remembers you."

Henri hesitated.

"Oh, I don't know."

He had not changed so much, he thought, from that shy twenty-year-old man.

Giselle showed him how to do it. All evening he dithered.

But then, somehow, he found his courage and sent a message to the lady he believed to be Louise.

He was so surprised when a message came straight back.

Oh, Henri! Is that really you?

They chatted online for over an hour, with Louise telling Henri all about her life. She had a son but was no longer married.

She was thrilled when he told her how successful he'd become.

"It is all thanks to you and your beautiful face," he said.

"Not so beautiful now." She laughed.

"It is."

He told her about the planned exhibition tour. When he said he was coming to England, she was excited.

Oh, Henri, please come and see me – if you've time.

I will make the time.

They agreed on a date and Henri started to count down the days.

*   *   *   *

After stepping off the train in Bournemouth, Henri told his agent he would meet him back at the hotel later.

"Don't forget we're staying at the Hotel Heritage near the seafront."

"I will remember. I am not that old." Henri laughed.

They said goodbye and Henri bought some flowers from the florist's by the station. He felt a mixture of nerves and excitement as he checked his appearance in the shop window.

His hair was grey now and lines criss-crossed the skin under his dark eyes.

What was he doing – acting like a teenager when he was an old man? Outside he found a taxi.

"Seventeen Woodcroft Road, please."

When the taxi driver dropped him off, he said, "Good luck."

Henri frowned.

"How do you know I need it?"

The man tapped the side of his nose.

"Taxi drivers pick up a lot. You've flowers and you wriggled around like you were sitting on an ant's nest. There's always a lady involved."

"You are right, my friend." Henri smiled as he paid him.

Walking along the row of identical terraces, he searched for number seventeen but before he could climb the steps to her apartment Louise, wearing a red dress and matching shoes, opened the door.

"Henri – you've not changed at all!" she exclaimed.

He could not believe he had not recognised her from her photographs. Louise was still as lovely as that first day in his studio.

His shyness forgotten, he handed her the flowers.

"To thank you. I owe you my career."

She hugged him.

"I'll put these in a vase then we'll go," she said.

"Where?" He was puzzled.

"Marmaduke's."

"It is still there? Our café?"

"Yes," she replied. "A bit more modern than when you last visited. I always think of you when I'm there."

He smiled as they walked along her road. When she linked her arm through his, he felt as if they'd never been apart.

Marmaduke's had indeed changed. It had been extended and now had an oak floor. The tables were covered in white linen and instead of a jukebox, soft music played.

But it still had the essence of the old café which warmed Henri's heart as much as it did to be with Louise again.

"What would you like?" he asked.

"Hot chocolate, of course."

Quietly, Louise told him a little of her life. How she'd married Phil, but his drinking had driven them apart.

"But I'm happy now. We had a wonderful son who has two little girls I see all the time."

It was then that Henri realised why he hadn't recognised her from the first photo. The sadness had disappeared from her eyes.

If he were to paint her again, he'd capture her perfectly.

"It's wonderful to see you again, Henri. We mustn't lose touch."

"Oh, we won't," he said, holding her hands. "We can't go back in life, but we can pick up where we left off." ∎

Vintage Cleaning Tips from the "Friend"

Plant Extracts

PLANT extracts are valued as natural cleaners in our modern, eco-conscious times. But they have been used for centuries to help keep our homes clean, hygienic and pest-free.

Salts of lemon was a popular stain remover at the turn of the century. Alternatively known as oxalic acid, it has nothing to do with lemons, but occurs naturally in many plants, including spinach, parsley and rhubarb leaves.

The white powder is a bleaching agent and also reacts with iron compounds, so is useful for removing rust and ink stains, as noted in a "Friend" tip of 1915, which advised that ink "stains on cotton goods need salts of lemon melted in boiling water."

Insecticides are very useful, especially in the summertime, but many are also toxic to humans or pets. Not so the bark of the quassia, or bitter-ash tree, which one 1921 reader recommended highly.

"When scrubbing floors, put quassia in the water," she wrote. "Wherever it is used, no fleas or other vermin or insects can live or come. Get 2 oz. at the chemist (called quassia chips), boil in a gallon of water about half an hour; use about 2 large teacupfuls in every bucket of water. Nothing is better for wooden bedsteads than to wipe them over with this solution."

Quassia is still valued for its medicinal and insecticidal properties and is used as a pesticide in organic farming.

Perhaps the most versatile plant extract was turpentine, from pine resin. It could be used for anything from glassware to floor care, and, in 1921, it was recommended as an air freshener!

"A large vessel containing water, to which has been added a few drops of turpentine, should always be kept near a gas fire. The atmosphere of the room is thereby kept fresh, the turpentine giving a faint but agreeable aroma."

Perhaps an open window would have been preferable! ■

An Empty Nest

by Lynne Hallett

CLAIRE sat looking at the blank Word document. The vertical line flashed repeatedly, with the regularity of a pulse.

She had stories to write and deadlines to meet, but her mind was elsewhere – approximately 170 miles away in York, wondering what Charlie would be doing now, and if he had managed to get himself up on time and to the relevant lectures.

The house was silent, save for the distant chugging of the washing machine.

Outside the birds were chirping, engaged in conversation with each other. Their apparent happiness only heightened her misery and isolation.

She glanced at the oak tree behind their garden fence. It was still full of leaves, though they were turning golden now. Soon they would fall, leaving the tree bare.

The garden retained the vestiges of summer colour, but its hold on the plants was weakening. They would shrivel and die.

Claire got up from her chair and went to the kitchen. Coffee and cake might lift her spirits.

She knew that she had a tendency to be more emotional when she was tired, so the caffeine and sugar might give her the zing she needed.

She mustn't mope. Tony was right when he said that university was where Charlie needed to be.

It was a natural progression, but she couldn't understand how he could be so matter of fact about it all. It was like he didn't care.

She'd spent a night tossing and turning, trying to sleep and failing. Tony had dropped off almost instantly and snored the hours away.

Claire returned to the conservatory and sat down at the desk, sipping her coffee. It was sweet and warming. She stared at the screen. The vertical line continued to flash.

"Come on," she told herself. "You just need to start typing. Anything will do. Just type some words."

She laid her fingers on the keys as a pianist might and typed out a sentence.

She paused, shook her head and deleted it. It was time for extreme measures.

She opened a drawer to her left, pulled out a beautiful journal and leafed through the collection of inspirational ideas.

When she had first started writing, she had followed advice to gather snippets of information, headlines, pictures from magazines, anything that might kickstart the imagination on a particularly difficult day.

From time to time she pulled it out, and it never failed. But nothing resonated today. Claire put it on the desk and finished her cake.

Maybe getting out would be a better idea and help to clear her mind.

Which of her friends would be most likely to drop everything and meet her for a walk?

Jo. She wasn't working at the moment and was always keen to get out, so Claire texted her.

As she expected, there was an almost instant response.

Will meet you in Priory Park with Sasha. She'll enjoy an extra walk. See you at eleven.

*   *   *   *

As Claire approached Jo, Sasha started to bark and strain at the lead. "She always loves seeing you. Don't you, Sasha?" Jo leaned forward and gave Claire a hug. "Let's walk and you can tell me all about it, whatever it is."

"I'm just being silly, really," Claire replied. "We took Charlie up to York yesterday."

"I see."

Claire nodded. She could feel her eyes welling with tears.

Jo put a comforting arm around her shoulders.

"Cry if you need to. It's OK. It's perfectly normal, lasts a few weeks and doesn't prove fatal – take it from me."

"I know all that, but I hadn't expected it to be so bad," Claire admitted. "I feel grief-stricken."

"Well, it is a loss of sorts."

"The house was so quiet this morning. Tony went to work and I sat down to write and, well, nothing happened."

"So?"

"I'm a writer, Jo. Writers need to write. I had no inspiration today," Claire explained.

"You haven't lost it, Claire. Well, not permanently anyway," Jo assured her. "You're just sad and a bit distracted. Be kinder to yourself. You have to adjust."

Claire shrugged.

"I'd expected that, but I think Tony has already adjusted. We came back last night after dropping Charlie off and he sat down on the sofa, put the telly on and said how happy he was that it was just him and me at last."

"Well, that's nice, isn't it?" Jo reasoned.

"In a way. But he obviously doesn't have the gaping hole inside that I do," Claire replied. "He doesn't understand.

"It's like he couldn't wait to be rid of him, and it got me wondering how long he's been feeling like that."

Jo smiled.

"I'm sure he's missing him, in his own way," she told her friend. "It is different for mums and dads. It certainly was for us."

"Was it?"

"Of course it was. I was a bit more like you. Dave just got on with it," Jo explained. "He missed Lizzie most when she went, though. Dads and daughters and all that. He worried about her a lot more, too."

"How did you cope?" Claire asked.

"I used to go into their rooms when they left and open the curtains and say out loud, 'Morning, love', and then in the evening I would close the curtains and wish them pleasant dreams.

Moments In Time

The frames are old and different shapes,
But somehow that's all right;
Some photos date back many years
In faded black and white.

My parents on their wedding day,
My mother's veil so fine;
How tall and proud my father stands,
Shoes blinding with their shine.

And here I am, a babe in arms,
Then schoolgirl meek and mild,
Now veiled in white, a blushing bride,
Then holding our first child.

And here, my children's wedding days,
Such joy but sadness, too –
That feeling that they've flown the nest
To start a life that's new.

So many loved ones, some long gone,
Time passes as it should;
My grandchildren will carry on –
The future's looking good!

Eileen Hay.

Shutterstock

"It got me over that hurdle. Before I knew it, they were back for the holidays, then there was another period of readjustment because we'd been used to having the house to ourselves," Jo finished.

Claire smiled.

"I hadn't thought about that."

"They're always in touch, you know – especially when they need money."

"You always know what to say, Jo." Claire's phone beeped and she pulled it from her pocket.

"Charlie?" Jo asked.

"No, Tony."

"You look puzzled."

"Yes. He's sent me a cryptic message: *Don't cook dinner tonight.*"

"What's cryptic about that?"

"Well, I always cook."

"Maybe he's made plans." Jo raised an eyebrow.

"Get away with you." Claire frowned. "It's always me who organises everything."

"He could be turning over a new leaf."

"We'll see." Claire was doubtful. "In the meantime, I shall enjoy this walk with you and Sasha."

"Good idea. Take today off and treat yourself."

*   *   *   *

By the time Claire got home, having had an extended lunch with Jo and a long chat, the weight in her chest had lifted somewhat.

She wandered to the laptop, opened it up, hesitated, shut it again, and picked up a book.

Immersed in the contents, she lost track of time and was surprised to hear the scraping of the key in the lock.

She walked through the living-room to the hall to find Tony holding a massive bouquet of flowers and a supermarket shopping bag.

The flowers were gorgeous, with all her favourites and in vibrant colours.

"For you, my darling," he said, handing her the flowers and giving her a kiss on the lips.

"They are lovely, but there was no need." Claire cradled the bouquet like a baby.

"I think there is. I know how hard it was for you to leave Charlie yesterday. It's only natural.

"He's our only one and you don't have your baby to fuss over any more, even if he's a rather big baby now," Tony acknowledged.

"I didn't think you understood."

"I know, but I'm trying. And to that end, I've bought a special dinner for two, so that you don't have to cook."

He headed to the kitchen and deposited the bag on the work surface.

"Oh, yes, and I mustn't forget this." Tony pulled out a bottle of champagne.

"But what are we celebrating?" Claire asked with a grin.

"We are celebrating being good parents and having given Charlie the best of starts," Tony replied. "We can celebrate the beginning of his new adventure – and ours, too.

"I won't lie. I've loved it being the three of us, and I wouldn't have had it any other way, but I have sometimes missed it being the two of us."

He looked at her, tilted his head slightly in that way he did, and smiled.

Her heart expanded. It hurt, but in a good way.

After dinner, she knew exactly what she was going to write about.

Well, maybe not after dinner. Maybe it could wait until the morning. ■

Norwich, Norfolk

The compact city of Norwich has a surprising amount of mediaeval churches, second only to London, in fact. Known for building its fortune from the wool trade, the city is steeped in history – such as its 900-year-old Norman castle in which Henry I spent Christmas in 1121. The Norman keep was given a facelift in the 1830s.

Norwich also boasts a surprising number of theatres for its size, and for those who love to delve into history, the Bridewell museum recounts the city's industrial heritage. It can lay claim to surprising things – postcodes were first trialled here and it is also home, of course, to Colman's Mustard – thanks to Jeremiah Colman's condiment created back in the early 1800s and still as popular today.

Norwich is a vibrant city with a large student population, so it's no surprise the average age of its citizens is a youthful thirty-seven. Take a stroll through the Royal Arcade – the creation of George Skipper – and if you fancy getting away from the hustle and bustle, have a stroll by the River Wensum.

Any Objections?

by Alyson Hilbourne

J ESS bent down to put another bucket between the chairs and looked up at the ceiling of the village hall in despair. Tell-tale brown stains showed the roof had been leaking for a while. If ever proof was needed that tonight's meeting was important, this was it, Jess thought.

"Oh, no. More leaks."

The voice made Jess look up. Jack Shepherd.

She gave a quick nod and pressed her lips together. Jack always came to the meetings and always had something to say. Jess had pegged him as somewhat opinionated.

He always seemed to have some disagreement with the plans the committee were putting forward and demanded to know every single detail of what was being proposed.

Jess sighed quietly. Still, he was always at the meetings and certainly showed an interest. He usually sat with some older members of the community and was possibly a representative of their views, which was odd because he was, like Jess, one of the younger residents in the village.

He had a car repair shop where the old petrol station used to be, but so far Jess had avoided taking her car there.

"Yes," she answered. "We need to get work started as soon as possible."

"You won't find me objecting," Jack said.

It was all Jess could do not to roll her eyes. All he ever seemed to do was object. She smiled insincerely and edged her way out from between the chairs.

The village needed to consent to a plan to renovate the hall. They had been raising money for the last five years but still hadn't agreed on a specific plan of work.

Meetings had gone round and round in circles with different proposals

Illustration by Mandy Murray.

put forward each time. In the end, driven by the indecision and lack of leadership, Jess had agreed to stand as chairperson of the committee overseeing the renovations.

She smiled as other people started arriving, glad of the diversion and distancing herself from Jack. More than once she thought he'd been watching her, both at the meetings and around the village.

She nodded to Oscar from the Red Lion and Mary, chief fund-raiser, as they shook umbrellas and shrugged off wet jackets.

"Filthy evening," someone called over to Jess.

The hall filled up with villagers and Jess could feel butterflies flitting about in her stomach. She wasn't used to public speaking.

Even knowing many of the people in the room didn't make it better.

She'd only taken the role of chairperson because she wanted to see a dynamic overhaul of the place, turning it into a building that would give the community a space for the future.

Some of the village residents, however, apparently led by Jack Shepherd, appeared to want the hall to remain firmly fixed in the past, with the minimum of work done to it.

It looked as if they were trying to spike all hope of progressing with the project.

She stood up and cleared her throat. Apart from the front row, no-one noticed and people carried on chatting to their neighbours, so Jess banged a teaspoon against her glass.

Immediately a hush fell over the hall and Jess's cheeks reddened.

"Good evening, everybody. I hope you've all had time to look at the architect's plans that have been posted on the noticeboard outside and were on the village website.

"The focus of tonight's meeting is to take a vote on the plan and decide the way forward. Now, does anybody have questions?"

"Where's the stage gone?" somebody shouted from the back. "Where will the children do their nativity play, and the choir perform?"

"If you look carefully," Jess said, "you'll see there is a retractable stage. It gives us more floor space for things like dances, fitness classes and craft fairs. The stage isn't used much but it can be pulled out if we need it."

The questioner appeared happy with that answer.

Jess looked across the hall and nodded at a raised hand. Then she saw whose hand it was.

She braced herself for an awkward question.

"What about the tea urn?"

Jess blinked in surprise.

"The tea urn will have loads of space in the extended kitchen, and with the rewiring it could be plugged in anywhere."

Jess looked across the sea of faces to Jack and saw him being nudged and whispered to by the elderly ladies who flanked him. He looked from one to the other and asked another question.

"Will there be hot water in the kitchen for washing up?"

"Of course," Jess said. "And there is under-the-counter space for a dishwasher, although we haven't budgeted for that yet, so it may have to wait."

The woman on one side of Jack appeared happy with that answer, but the one on the other side thinned her lips, folded her arms across her chest and whispered something else to Jack.

He cleared his throat.

"If there isn't a stage any more, where will the storage be? Where will the Christmas decorations be put, for example?"

The little group of people around Jack were all whispering to each other and pointing and pulling to attract each other's attention.

Did Jack think no-one had thought about these things? Jess couldn't help feeling his group were just stirring up trouble.

"The store room is still there for chairs and tables when they are not in use, and if you look there will be some attic storage over the extended kitchen and bathroom – perhaps not quite as convenient as under the stage but just as spacious."

Jack gave a smile and a nod and turned to his neighbours while Jess answered more questions from other people.

As the questions slowed, she introduced the architect, who explained what the building process would be.

After an hour or more she saw people were beginning to get fidgety. "If there are no more questions?" She glanced around, avoiding eye contact with Jack, who looked as if he might be about to ask something further.

"Right, if everyone is happy we'll take a vote. All those in favour of the architect's plans, raise your hand."

Almost every hand in the hall was raised and the vote was carried overwhelmingly. Jess breathed a sigh of relief.

"Right," she said. "I'll get things rolling. Remember we still need to do some fund-raising. Mary is in charge."

Jess nodded at the older woman in jeans and sweatshirt who sat next to her.

"Please go to her with any ideas. The lottery money has given the fund a huge boost but there are bound to be unforeseen expenses. The work should take three months once it starts so I'm afraid the hall will be out of commission for a while.

"The vicar has kindly offered the mother and toddler group space at the back of the church for a few weeks, and evening events can be booked in the school gym." She looked down at her list.

"Final item. Does anyone have any ideas for a reopening?"

"Someone famous to cut the ribbon?" someone said.

"That writer chappie?" someone else suggested.

Jess raised an eyebrow.

"Who is that?"

"Oh, I can't remember his name," the speaker said.

"How about Matthew Lung?" Jack's voice cut through the discussions in the hall. "He lives in the next village."

"The actor?" Jess said. "I didn't know he lived nearby. That's a good idea. I wonder if he'd be up for it. Shall we take a vote? All in favour?"

Hands shot up all round.

"Right. I'll get in touch with his agent." Jess made a note on the pad in front of her. "What do you think? Coffee morning, afternoon −"

"Bingo night?" It was Jack's voice again and met with hoots of laughter.

Jess flushed with annoyance. He should try being up here instead of making difficulties all the time. It was like trying to herd ants.

"Perhaps we can decide on an event when we have a finishing date for the work," she said diplomatically. "Unless there is anything else . . .?"

Chairs scraped and people began chatting together. Jess gathered her papers together, too. Well, it hadn't been as bad as she'd expected. At least the work could start now.

Jess watched as everyone left the hall and then began collecting up the chairs and pulling them to the side.

"Sorry!" A voice made her jump. "I'd have stayed to help, but I had to get Gran and Auntie Ivy home."

Jess straightened up and stared in surprise at Jack.

"It's OK. Done now," she mumbled.

"Look, I'm sorry about the questions." Jack leaned on a chair.

"Auntie Ivy wanted me to ask about the urn. She's manned it for all sorts of events over the years, apparently. She thinks of it as hers."

Jess relaxed a little. He hadn't come to pick a fight, at least.

"I didn't know that was your grandmother and aunt," she said.

Jack looked down at the ground and then up at Jess again.

"Yes. I moved to the village to be near them. I had so many good memories of staying here when I was a kid."

"The bingo night?" Jess asked.

"Ah, yes. That was Gran. See, she and her sister have lived in the village all their lives. They saw the village hall being built just after the war, replacing the Nissen hut that was here before.

"And back in the Seventies they loved the bingo nights that used to run. They don't want change. Well, not much. Maybe the dishwasher."

He grinned, two dimples denting his cheeks, and this time Jess saw a smile rather than a smirk.

She stared at him for a moment and ran a hand across her chin.

"I thought they were being deliberately difficult," she said. "Surely they can see we need something more modern with better facilities? The village is much bigger than it used to be, for a start."

"I know, I know." Jack held up his hands. "But they are rather stuck in their ways now and tend to look back to the old days fondly."

"The old days?" Jess said slowly. "What about a wartime-themed dance to celebrate the reopening of the hall?" she asked. "We could have fancy dress and a band and decorate the hall with flags."

She looked at Jack questioningly.

"Would that appeal to those who remember the hall opening the first time?"

"It might." Jack nodded. "Yes, it might."

*   *   *   *

The idea of a dance to reopen the hall was put on the agenda for the next meeting, which was held in the Red Lion since the hall was out of use.

Meanwhile, the builders had started work, and Jess had put aside the files of plans and settled back to her own job, designing greetings cards and painting landscapes.

As the meeting got started Jess stood up to give a report on the progress.

"I can tell you that the new wall has been built to extend the kitchen and bathrooms. The roof has been insulated, and the corrugated metal is going on this week.

"It's all on schedule. The kitchen roof, fixtures and fittings, new windows and floor and the stage are all lined up for the next month."

People nodded as Jess explained what was going on.

She then tentatively suggested the idea of a wartime dance for the reopening of the hall.

There was an immediate buzz of conversation. Jess watched, and on the whole concluded people looked as if they thought it was a good idea.

"Can we take a vote?" she called when the idea had been mulled over. It was passed convincingly and Jess managed to get a group of volunteers to organise it.

"I've spoken to Matthew Lung and he's agreed to come and open the hall," she said. "He is quite happy to dress in uniform for the dance."

* * * *

Two months later the renovations had been signed off by the builders and it was the evening of the dance.

The committee had decorated the hall with Union Jack flags, taped up the windows against bomb damage, and put sandbags round the door.

The lighting was dimmed and a glitter ball splashed spots of colour across the floor.

"It's wonderful," Jess said when she was shown round.

Oscar from the Red Lion was running a bar, the WI had prepared food and Mary had sold lots of tickets in advance.

Now Jess stood outside the hall listening to the four-piece band tuning up and waiting for Matthew Lung to arrive.

She smoothed down her frock, rented from the fancy dress shop in town, and touched her mouth — the lipstick felt odd.

"You look grand!" Jack sauntered over. "And the hall is fabulous. They've done a great job, thanks to you."

"Thank you." Jess looked down. She still wasn't sure if Jack was being genuine or not. "We still need to raise funds," she added.

"It'll come," Jack said. "Now the hall is looking good, folk will want to hire it."

Jess glanced at her watch and frowned. Then her phoned beeped. She opened her clutch bag and listened to the voicemail message.

"No!"

Jack looked at her and arched an eyebrow.

"Matthew Lung has had a fall, just as he was on his way. His wife has taken him to A and E with a suspected broken leg. What am I going to do?" Jess's voice rose to a wail.

"You could do it," Jack said.

Jess looked at him in horror.

"No, no. It needs to be someone proper. They don't want me again."

"Hold on." Jack touched her arm but Jess didn't notice. "I've an idea."

He ran off, shouting over his shoulder, "Don't do anything. I'll be back soon," leaving Jess standing helplessly in the car park.

She gritted her teeth and waved at people as they walked up to the door to show their tickets. She could see people had made an effort to dress up, but she feared the opening was going to be a let-down.

Jack needed to be quick.

She wandered across the car park and peered out into the road. There was no sign of him.

Ten minutes later, just as Jess thought she'd have to go inside and say something herself, Jack came back, walking slowly, an old lady holding each arm.

"Sorry," he said. "They wanted a few minutes to put their glad rags on. I give you the oldest residents of the village, who remember the hall being built: Gran and Auntie Ivy. Perhaps they could open it?"

Jess clapped her hands.

"Brilliant," she said. "Good thinking."

They all went inside. Jack stood at the microphone and introduced Ann Shepherd and Ivy Cook.

"I remember when the hall was first built," Ivy said. "Over the years it has been used for all sorts of things.

"As well as shows and dances, fairs and yoga, it's been a refuge in time of flood, a field hospital during a measles epidemic and a home to refugees."

Jess's eyes widened. She'd had no idea.

Ann then spoke.

"It's so good to see the hall renovated so the next generation can enjoy it. It does look good." She looked up at the ceiling, freshly painted. "But . . ."

Jess's heart sank. Was she still arguing? What wasn't she happy about now?

"We still need to raise funds – we need that dishwasher!" Ann finished.

People laughed and Jess heard a wolf whistle.

"So I propose a bingo night." Ann raised a hand in the air.

There were raucous cheers and a ripple of applause as people raised their glasses to the renovated hall.

Then the band started up and the first couples got up to the dance floor.

Jess sank down in a chair and relaxed.

Jack settled his gran and aunt at a table and came over.

"Gran and Auntie are very happy," he said. "I know they weren't convinced by the changes but I think you've got their grudging approval."

Jess looked up and smiled.

"That's good," she said. "Asking them to open the dance was a stroke of genius. Thank you for that. It really got me out of a hole."

"You're welcome," Jack said. "But Gran's not going to give up, you know. She wants a bingo night."

"Not my problem any more." Jess laughed. "My job finished with the opening of the hall."

"Oh, darn," Jack said, a smile playing at the edge of his mouth. "I was looking forward to chasing you up about that."

Jess looked at him sharply.

"You mean you've been deliberately winding me up?"

"Only on Gran's behalf," Jack said. "But I have to say it's been an excellent opportunity to get to know you. You handle her very well. She's quite won over. As am I. Would you honour me with a dance?"

As Jess stood up and moved on to the dance floor, she wondered if perhaps her first impressions of Jack had been too harsh.

Maybe he wasn't always argumentative . . . she'd just have to see. ∎

Vintage Cleaning Tips from the "Friend"

Glycerine

GLYCERINE is a colourless, thick, sweet-tasting liquid. It occurs naturally in many plant oils and much is produced as a by-product of soap-making or from the production of biodiesel. It can also be made synthetically.

A type of alcohol, it has antimicrobial and antiviral properties, so has been used in clinical settings for treating wounds and burns. Most households would have had a bottle of glycerine in store, because it was used for soothing coughs and sore throats.

But glycerine has another advantage, in that it mixes well with water, which makes it very useful for removing stains. In 1955, the "Friend" gave readers a whole host of useful tips for how to use it.

One handy hint concerned how to deal with tired bedding.

"Remove grease stains from blankets by rubbing glycerine thickly over the spots. Leave for an hour, then sponge with ammonia and water. Make a ring of powdered magnesia round the stain to keep the glycerine from spreading."

It's good at keeping windows from steaming up, too.

"To prevent windows from steaming, first clean in the usual way and dry properly, giving a final polish with a soft cloth. Then moisten a clean cloth with a few drops of glycerine and rub well over the glass."

Mirrors could be given the glycerine treatment. "To prevent a mirror from clouding, rub it with a cloth wrung out of hot water and sprinkled with glycerine. The glycerine forms a thin film on the glass."

It could even help to release stuck glass.

"When a glass stopper is stuck fast, pour a little glycerine round the neck and let it stand until the stopper will lift out easily."

This last tip makes use of glycerine's properties as an excellent moisturising agent – the reason why it is to be found as an ingredient in many toiletries and skin care products. Not only can it help around the house, it can even soften and soothe your hands after you've finished all the chores! ■

Shutterstock.

Hearts Of Oak

by Julie Goodall

AUTUMN 2010. This is all so weird, Ade. It's changed so much. One-way streets. The town has been pedestrianised." Sally changed down a gear and slowed for the left turn that the GPS on her phone indicated.

"I think the park was just around about here." Adrian leaned forward in his seat, confusion narrowing his eyes. "Hold on . . . what are all these houses?"

Sally sighed and slowed down to first.

"A new estate?"

Checking her mirrors, she drew to a halt and parallel parked between two cars. When she exchanged glances with her husband, there was silent agreement to go and explore.

The wind almost took Sally's breath away and she grasped Adrian's hand. Together they walked up the street, taking in the new surroundings. Nothing remained of the park they'd once known so well.

"Surely you can't just demolish it?" Adrian mused, dropping her hand to scroll on his phone. "You have to provide green spaces. I'm pretty sure it's the law.

"Yep, look . . ." He moved the phone so that Sally could see the screen. "They must have knocked down the old warehouses on the way to the quarry. There's a park there now."

Looking around, Sally's heart sank. They'd been so looking forward to this visit, reliving old memories, seeing old haunts again. Of course, the tree had been the most poignant of them all.

"It still feels quite green here, though," she commented, trying her best to be positive. "They appear to have made an effort to keep it as natural as possible. They've even named the streets after the trees."

Adrian peered at his phone and read out a few names: Elm Close, Hawthorn Lane, Oak Road. Sally caught his eye.

"Oak Road? How far is that?"

Illustration by Shutterstock.

He pointed, a small, hopeful glint in his eyes.

"Left at the next turning, then along a bit and right."

Striding off, they arrived at Oak Road and Sally's heart sank.

"I can't believe it. I was so looking forward to walking through the park and sitting under our tree."

"I know, love. Me, too. Nice houses, though," he added, his sweeping arm taking them in. "Upmarket. At least they built something people might be happy to live in, I suppose."

"I guess." Frustrated by the wind, Sally stopped for a moment to search for a hairband in her handbag.

"There's an alleyway here!" Adrian called, having gone on ahead. "It might go round the back of the gardens. Shall we have a nose?"

Sally nodded, catching up.

They waded through fallen leaves that had drifted from various gardens. It was a bit of a labyrinth.

The alleyway turned into a crossroads and there was a quick discussion as to which part of the park they could have been in, but it was impossible to know with any certainty.

With no reference marker, they could have been anywhere . . . by the swings, by the mound that they'd run up and down as children, by the ice-cream parlour and toilet block.

Then something caught Adrian's eye. Sally saw him straighten then hurry ahead.

"Wait for me!" she called, and was intrigued to find him standing on tiptoe. When he turned, his face, still tanned from the late summer heatwave, beamed from ear to ear.

"Look!"

She did look and couldn't believe what she saw. At the foot of a garden, with some of the branches overhanging the alleyway, was the old oak tree. It wasn't just any tree – she knew that straight away. The shape of it was unmistakeable.

They peered over the fence like naughty schoolchildren hoping to scrump apples. But it was the sweetness of memories they sought, not fruit.

She felt Adrian's hand warm in hers.

"It's still here," he whispered.

"And so are we," she replied.

*   *   *   *

Autumn 1980.

Adrian watched with horror as Bowie raced over the grass towards the girls beneath the tree. He didn't need a crystal ball to know what was about to follow.

A plate sat beside their tiny barbecue and the meat on it was about to disappear faster than water down a plughole.

Bowie had form and he'd take no prisoners, pretty females or otherwise.

"Bowie!" he yelled in panic.

As expected, the dog turned not a single hair.

The embarrassment hit a level hitherto unreached when Bowie flew back and deposited a charred sausage at Adrian's feet. Bending to retrieve it, the blood flooded Adrian's face.

"I'm so sorry," he panted, aware that he had been watched for the whole of his approach to the foot of the tree. The girls were doubled up with laughter as he dangled the sausage out of the dog's reach.

Bowie jumped up repeatedly but Adrian refused to give in.

"He's a nightmare. In the summer, I keep him on a lead, but I didn't expect anyone to be barbecuing at this time of year.

"Can I get you some chips from the takeaway to make up for it? It's not the same, I know . . ."

A girl with long, flaming red hair held up a hand, apparently still unable to speak, shaking her head. Finally she got her breath back.

"It's fine," she gasped out. "It was honestly worth it to see the look on your face."

"Let him eat it," the other girl said, pointing at Bowie. "He's earned it, I'd say!"

They laughed again, until the redhead pulled herself together.

Frozen Moment

It's a morn for believing in fairies,
A magical chill nips the air,
The world has been sprinkled with stardust
Sparkling white everywhere.

Each frosted crystal's a wonder
But such fragile beauty can't stay,
There won't be a trace left by lunchtime,
Enjoy it all now, while you may.

Laura Tapper.

Shutterstock.

"Love the name, by the way."

"The name? Oh, Bowie. Ha. Yes. My idol."

"Mine, too. I'm Sally."

Adrian looked at her with increased interest. Beautiful and a Bowie fan. Perhaps this was actually his lucky day.

* * * *

Autumn 1984.

Adrian couldn't help but wonder if it was supposed to be quite like this. He'd felt sick for a week and, last night, sleep had eluded him. Today he'd managed some toast for breakfast but hadn't eaten a morsel for the rest of the day.

"I thought you were taking me somewhere special?" Sally mused, as he took her hand and led her into the park. "I've got myself all dressed up."

"I am taking you somewhere special," he replied, squeezing her hand to reassure her. "And you look stunning. I've got myself dressed up, too."

He dropped her hand and did a comical twirl to reinforce his point.

"I do like you in a suit."

He didn't fail to miss her flirty tone and grinned in response.

Before long, they were at the oak tree.

"Ha! I remember this! Your naughty dog, Bowie. He hasn't changed one bit."

'Nor have you," Adrian said, his hand trembling through his hair. "And that's why we're here. I've realised that I would never want you to change, and I love every bit of you.

"It was here that I first laid eyes on you. You chose this tree that day to give you shelter. Today I choose this tree to remind us that good things grow from roots, but the roots need to be strong.

"If they are, then what comes after is healthy and vibrant. I want us to reach out into the world with our own branches, Sally. Furnish the world with our own little twigs."

Sally looked astonished.

"Ade, are you OK?"

"Let me finish. It's important."

Rarely silenced, Sally let him go on.

"I want us to be like this trunk, solid and strong, battling through every season. I know we'll have our winters. It's inevitable that we will. Our leaves will probably drop and we will feel we have been laid bare.

"But we'll relish the springs and the summers. Together we can colour the world with our combined shades."

Sally giggled nervously.

"Have you swallowed a poetry book?"

Fumbling in his pocket, Adrian lowered to one knee.

"Sally, will you do me the honour of being my wife?"

The open box sat on his palm and Sally stared inside.

"Do you honestly need to ask? Of course I'll marry you!"

As her trembling hand reached out to take the ring, a lone yellow leaf floated down from above and landed in the box.

✳   ✳   ✳   ✳

Autumn 2020.

"This was a perfect idea."

"I'm full of them. Always have been. That's why you married me."

Sally laughed.

"No, I'm serious. Putting the swing here. I love it. Now we don't only get to look at the tree . . . we can sort of be part of it. I still miss Bowie, you know."

"The dog or the human?"

"Both, really."

Adrian nodded.

"Me, too. I suppose we could get another one. Dog, I mean."

"You're right. Now the kids have all gone and we're both working part time, I think we'd have time for one again."

They sat for a while, looking down the garden at their new house.

"I still can't believe that this place came up for sale." Sally looked at him, as if hoping for the answer to their little miracle.

"I've had an alert on the estate agent's website for a few years," Adrian said. "Lots of others came up, and I always had to study the photos to see if it was this one.

"It was the tree, of course, in the garden, that confirmed it. Every time I had an alert, my heart missed a beat."

Sally thought that he still made her heart miss a beat, even after all this time.

"You sneaky . . . you never said you'd been looking for so long!" she exclaimed.

The swing tilted as he slipped off it and reached down behind the tree trunk.

"I've got something for you," he said. He handed her a piece of laminated plastic, but there was something inside. "I pressed it, at first, but eventually I had it laminated. It's lost most of its colour, but there's a tiny bit left."

"A leaf?" Sally took it, confused.

"*The* leaf. The one that landed in the box."

"Oh, my goodness! You kept it! You really are full of surprises."

She held the laminated leaf up to the watery sunshine.

"It's so pretty. How strange, to think that it came from this very tree, and how many leaves have replaced it over the years."

"That may be, but no-one will ever replace you."

Sally laughed again, leaning forward for a kiss.

"You really are turning into an old romantic in your dotage. Whatever brought this on?"

Adrian's gaze softened.

"I suppose it's the idea of things being renewed. Our tree is renewed every year, as is all nature, really. Digging out the leaf made me think of it.

"It's thirty-six years since I gave you the engagement ring and I wondered if it was time to renew our own wedding vows?"

Sally felt his hand slip into hers. She looked at the leaf and the veins that ran through it, at one time transporting food, water and minerals.

They were intricate and beautiful, spreading away from the main vein, reminding her of the paths she and Adrian had taken together in life. They had branched out as a couple, choosing routes that would enrich their family.

The storms of life had challenged them, but they had survived, although their colours, too, had been a touch faded at times.

"I would love to renew my vows," she confirmed, closing her eyes as he reached over to kiss her. Above, in their tree, a bird sang its tiny heart out. It was perched in its nest, claiming its patch, nestled in its home.

And sitting on the swing, beneath the tree that had given them such precious memories, Sally knew that she had been lucky.

They had lived in so many places, known so many people, and now, they had found somewhere really special to live.

Yet, despite that, she knew that, no matter where Adrian was, so long as she could be with him, she would always be home. ▥

Hallowe'en With Harvey

by Eirin Thompson

I F there was one time of year that was even busier than Christmas at Bird's Party Shop, then that time was Hallowe'en.

This was the season when the bell over the door chimed constantly, as customers piled in to buy or hire their fancy-dress costumes, wigs, fangs and fake blood.

"Do you have a Bart Simpson false face?" a harried-looking young mum enquired. "It's the only one my son wants."

"No problem," Emma replied. "We have the cheaper plastic one, or a more expensive version that'll last a lot longer."

Emma dressed as a witch for work throughout the month of October. It had been Mr Bird's suggestion, and he paid for a top-quality costume.

"It helps put customers in the mood for dressing up," he told her. "You know and I know, Emma, that for ten months of the year, this shop barely pays the rent.

"We need the tills full at Hallowe'en and Christmas to keep the business afloat."

Not that Emma needed any persuading to don a costume. She'd been coming to Bird's Party Shop for her outfits for as long as she could remember.

She was in her element, helping customers find masks, witches' hats and broomsticks, and less creepy sets, such as cowboys and mermaids.

Trade had built nicely in the first three weeks of the month. Emma and her older colleague, Theresa, had been busy, but coping.

Then Mr Bird arrived at the shop with the news that Theresa was unwell and needed a few days off work.

"Rotten timing, but all is not lost," Mr Bird told an anxious Emma. "I've drafted in my grandson, Harvey. He's between projects at the moment, so he has some time on his hands.

"You can show him the ropes and train him up to make himself useful."

Emma couldn't think of a worse week to try to train a new member of staff.

Illustration by Sarah Holliday.

"When does he arrive?" she enquired.

Mr Bird glanced at his watch.

"Actually, I thought he'd be here by now. I asked him to meet me at nine o'clock."

Emma wasn't impressed that her new helper showed no sign of being punctual on his first day.

*　*　*　*

It was almost ten o'clock when Harvey finally put in an appearance.

"Hi. I'm Harvey Bird. You must be Emily," he began.

"It's Emma, actually," Emma answered coolly. "Your grandad said you'd be here at nine. He's had to leave to see to some other matters."

"Nine o'clock? Oops. But I don't expect you get many customers that early, do you?"

"At this time of year people pop in all the time. As well as which, I need to keep moving the merchandise from the stock room to the shelves – I can't do that if it means leaving the shop unattended."

"Well, I'm here now. What can I do to help?"

Emma sighed.

"I suppose you should take a good look around the shop to familiarise yourself with our products. As least then you can help customers find what they're looking for."

While Harvey explored the shop-floor, Emma was able to make several trips to the stock room, bringing back items to refill the shelves.

After half an hour of this, plus Emma stopping to assist occasional customers, Harvey said, "OK, Emily, I think I'm ready."

"Ready for what? And it's Emma, not Emily."

"Ready for you to test me, of course. Ask me anything – anything about what we sell in this shop, that is."

Giving Harvey a merchandise quiz wasn't such a bad idea.

"All right. I want to go to a party dressed as a witch's cat. What can you provide?"

"A witch's cat? Yes, over here we have complete outfits, including black full-body leotard, face mask with whiskers, hair band with ears and attachable tail. Does that sound like what you were looking for?"

"That sounds excellent. However, it's a little over my budget – what can you do for under twenty quid?"

"Well, for the customer on a prudent budget, we can suggest you dress all in black and add just the ears and tail, which we can supply separately.

"We can also offer a face-painting palette for two pounds, which would enable you to paint on your own nose and whiskers."

Emma had to admit that Harvey's advice was good.

"All right. Since we're not too busy right now, let's put you on the till."

The pair stood side by side behind the counter as customers trickled in. Harvey made a few mistakes, but Emma was on hand to correct them.

"You're doing very well," she told him during a lull. "You're a quick learner."

"How come you're available, though, if you don't mind me asking?"

"Oh, I made a bit of a hash of going to university. I thought I knew what I wanted, but when I got there it just wasn't me."

"So you dropped out?"

"That makes me sound flaky – I prefer to say I had a change of direction."

Emma was less than impressed. She'd applied for university and worked her socks off to get the necessary grades, but she hadn't quite made it.

The thought that someone would take up a desirable uni place and then just walk away appalled her.

"So how long do you plan to work here?" she asked frostily, wondering if he would hang around long enough to cover for Theresa.

"Oh, this job's a keeper," he replied.

"I don't think so," Emma challenged him. "There really isn't enough work for three people."

"But we aren't three – there are just two of us."

"You're forgetting Theresa."

"Theresa's not coming back. She's decided to retire. Actually, Grandad told me not to say anything about that just yet, so don't tell him I told you – OK?"

Emma was stunned. Theresa often talked about wanting to spend more time with her grandchildren and on her allotment, but she'd never actually spoken in terms of retirement!

"So it's going to be just you and me from now on?"

Emma couldn't help rolling her eyes.

∗   ∗   ∗   ∗

"Grandad said we'd be rushed off our feet, but I wouldn't exactly call this busy," Harvey observed as lunchtime approached.

"I don't understand it – this should be our best week of the year, but it's been really quiet," Emma replied. "Take a look outside and check the pavement hasn't been dug up or something – that's all we'd need."

Harvey disappeared for a moment, then bounded back in.

"No roadworks, but I think I've detected the problem," he said. "Come and look."

There, straight across the road, in a building that had been vacant the last time she'd paid any attention to it, was a huge poster in the window, proclaiming: *Pop-up Hallowe'en Shop. Prices slashed!*

Outside, a queue had formed.

∗   ∗   ∗   ∗

Emma and Harvey were standing at the window, sipping their mugs of tea.

"I possibly shouldn't be sharing this with you, but who else can I talk to?" Emma began. "Not to put too fine a point on it, but if your grandad's shop doesn't have a boom for Hallowe'en, then I don't see it surviving.

"Honestly, there should be a law against opportunistic vendors who spring up for a week or two, take the money and run – never minding whom they've put out of a permanent job in the meantime."

"It does seem a bit unfair," Harvey agreed. "I mean, Grandad pays rent and rates and provides a service all year round – it's not a level playing field if someone else is happy just to make a quick buck and then scarper."

"I love this job," Emma told him. "When I didn't get into uni, I was so grateful that Mr Bird offered me the chance to go full time.

"I like chatting to the customers and hearing all about their party plans, and I love the children coming in full of excitement for their outfits.

"I'd miss all that so much if the shop closed."

"Then defeat isn't an option," Harvey pronounced. "We're going to have to figure out a way to get our till chiming. I have an idea."

∗   ∗   ∗   ∗

Emma stood behind the counter, watching the local news on the staff-room television through the open door.

"And now here's a film we made earlier at the famous Bird's Party Shop," the newsreader announced, "where Harvey Bird has transformed the premises with a startling array of life-size balloon models for Hallowe'en.

"Harvey, you've got Dracula, Frankenstein, witches and wizards. Where did you learn to make such incredible models?"

Harvey grinned.

"I attended a circus school in my gap year before university, where I learned to juggle, unicycle and stilt-walk, as well as balloon sculpture.

"In fact, I enjoyed myself so much that I decided I'd join the family firm, learn the business side and bring my circus skills to the set-up."

"So, Harvey – how can the public view these remarkable sculptures?"

"They're all on display in Bird's Party Shop – just call in. While you're there, we hope you'll also inspect our huge range of fancy-dress costumes and party pranks."

Emma left the counter to turn off the TV set.

Harvey had played a blinder, getting the balloons on television – but would the public come? By lunchtime, they had their answer.

There was a queue outside Bird's and the shop was packed with people. Harvey supervised the shop floor, answering queries, locating just the right items, and Emma rang it all up on the till.

At a quarter to three things suddenly went quiet, and a glance across the road showed no signs of any queue at the competition's premises.

"We'll have the best part of an hour to rest and tidy up the stock before it starts again," Emma assured Harvey.

She put on the kettle and they plonked themselves down in the little staff-room, door ajar so they would notice if someone entered the shop.

"That was brilliant!" Harvey said with a wide smile.

"It was," Emma agreed. "And it's all down to you. You must have been up all night, modelling those balloons."

"Pretty much," Harvey conceded. "Did you see the huge bags under my eyes when I was being interviewed?"

"No. I didn't. I saw a bright young man who is going to take the family business to the next level. I've never met anyone with circus skills."

"I'd quite like to be a clown, I think. I like making people smile."

"You could dress up as one, when you're working here – it could be our trademark."

It struck her that, with Harvey arriving on the scene, she might find new and wider opportunities within the business, too.

Perhaps university wouldn't have been the best path for her after all.

"Next Hallowe'en, we should organise our own fancy-dress ball," Harvey suggested, his eyes glistening with excitement.

"We could hire a venue, book a band and sell tons of costumes to the party-goers. We could have food and fireworks – I might have learned fire-eating by then . . ."

"Sounds great. But for the next ten minutes, can we just sit here? Otherwise I don't think I can keep up."

"Sure – Emma. See, I'm learning."

"Thank you, Harvey. And I might not have made it to uni, but since meeting you, I can honestly say I'm learning, too." ■

Vintage Cleaning Tips from the "Friend"

Paraffin

DISTILLED from coal or crude oil, paraffin — also known as kerosene — can dissolve grease, so was often used for washing heavily soiled items. Domestic manuals of the time advised caution, insisting that items laundered with paraffin be thoroughly rinsed and dried outdoors or, where this was not possible, by an open window — and well away from the fire!

Despite risk of fire, until the mid-20th century there were numerous tips attesting to paraffin's power to restore shine to glass and metals.

A tip in 1915 read, "Brass curtain rings that have been neglected may be cleaned by soaking them in paraffin for 24 hours and then polishing with ordinary brass paste. They will look like new."

Let's hope the weather in 1921 was warm enough to keep the windows open during spring-cleaning, as readers that year were encouraged to make liberal use of the pungent fluid.

"Mirrors," the "Friend" said, "must be kept bright, also glass of pictures, and a very simple method is to moisten a cloth with paraffin and go over the surface, then polish with a piece of fine linen. Paraffin gives a brilliancy to glass and mirrors which lasts well and resists dust better than if the surface were cleaned with water. Paraffin is also useful for cleaning dark wood-work and the smell will soon wear off if the windows be opened."

It was even recommended for everyday cleaning.

"No housewife who has tried the labour-saving virtues of an oiled duster in cleaning time would care to be without one of these useful cleaning articles. You can easily make them yourself.

"Get a piece of ordinary soft cloth, soak it in paraffin, then wring it out; now dry the duster out of doors, and the unpleasant smell will vanish. You will find that it gathers up all the dust instead of making it fly about the room, besides giving a brilliant polish to mirrors and glass globes, which should be rubbed afterwards with a clean, soft cloth. It also keeps flies from settling on the glass." Phew! ■

Shutterstock.

A Rising Star

======================= by Alison Carter =======================

T was going to be quiet in the theatre that night, and not just because thick, wet snow was coating London and muffling all sound. There was a theatre strike on – one of those small, short strikes that never really goes anywhere.

It meant that the front-of-house team was absent, so Bella would have plenty of time to put the finishing touches on "Snow And Show Tunes", a Christmas offering that was rather better than its title.

The strike meant that almost all the theatres in London would be dark for days, and the "Oklahoma!" style cowboy musical currently on at the Classic – Bella's theatre – would have a hole in its income.

But by now, in the last months of 1959, Bella had years of experience under her belt and knew that the Classic – and all the other theatres that put on great musicals – would survive.

She was in her office marking up a script when the phone rang.

"Bella? I tried you at home but as usual you're at work." It was Bella's sister Frances, a housewife with teenage children, living in Berkshire.

"I'd love to chat," Bella said, "but I've a lot on."

"I just need to tell you the result of the auction," Frances said. "Got a pencil?"

"Auction?" Bella imagined porcelain, or walnut bureaux.

"You offered a day backstage, remember? The event was in the village hall yesterday."

This was typical of Frances. In her sedate rural life this would have loomed large, whereas Bella's life really was busy.

Frances would expect Bella to remember when the residents of Little Wasthorpe would gather to swap jars of jam.

"People bid on lots that were work or help," Frances went on. "My friend Chloda bought three hours' ironing – bliss!"

"I have the name of the person who will be coming to you tomorrow.

"I'm going to meet her at the station with sandwiches, because she hasn't a bean and her mother won't remember."

Now Bella recalled a family supper in October at which Frances had

Set in 1959

Illustration by Kirk Houston.

nagged her for an auction offering.

She'd resisted, and their father had waded in.

"Come on, Bella," he said. "Can you imagine how much some young person would love to see all the props and scenery?"

Their father had frowned.

"It's something you can offer, Bella, and it's for a good cause ."

"Tomorrow?" Bella said into her office phone. "Can I delay it?"

Tomorrow would be easy, with only Bella and her assistant Charlie in the theatre, but the last thing she wanted was some eager citizen of Little Wasthorpe tailing after her.

"You cannot," Frances replied.

In her voice was some of the edge that Bella had been scared of when she was eight.

"I have a pencil," Bella said with a sigh.

The winner of the auction appeared at the stage door of the Classic the following day at three-thirty.

Charlie fetched her and presented her in the office.

"Maureen Godbolt," he said with a certain grandeur.

Maureen Godbolt, Bella thought – even the name didn't inspire confidence.

"Where shall we start?" Charlie asked.

Bella took a deep breath. If she was quick, Maureen might be on a train by five.

"Welcome, Maureen," she said. "I bet you'd like to see the place where Anna Neagle stashed her flowers after standing ovations?"

Maureen said she didn't mind what was first. She added that she didn't mind what she saw and was just glad to be there.

She was so over-excited that she made Bella feel tired.

"I've thought about drama school," Maureen told her as she followed Bella and Charlie along the back of the stage, a little too close and very much too talkative.

"But it's so expensive and you never know what will come of it," she continued. "Nobody in my family has ever been to a college or a university!"

She spoke in exclamation marks and giggled a lot. Bella tried hard not to find her irritating, and kept thinking of her waiting work.

After a while Charlie took Maureen off to make a cup of tea, thrilling her as they went with a tale that was well known at the Classic – an unexpected visit from Herbert Lom in 1954.

"He wanted a bag of sugar to take back to the kitchen at Drury Lane," Charlie explained.

"He didn't?" the girl cried.

"I'm not sure I believe it," Charlie admitted as they receded down the corridor.

Maureen returned wide-eyed and began fresh declarations of gratitude.

Bella watched her sip the tea and wondered if she had any talent, then reminded herself that one never really knew.

Charlie took Bella aside when Maureen was examining the costumes store.

"She spent every penny she had on that auction bid," he said.

"She works in a telephone exchange for a pittance. Her father died in Italy in the war."

"In that case I'm glad we're giving her the full tour," Bella replied.

"She has a heartfelt hope that she'll somehow make connections in the world of musical theatre while she's here. It's sweet."

Bella shook her head.

"So many have that hope," she said dryly.

"They deserve to dream. We should treat her."

"What do you mean?" Bella lowered her voice.

Maureen could be heard making her way back from the costumes store.

"Supper before she heads back?"

"That will prolong the agony."

Charlie looked stern.

"Bella," he scolded. "We can take her to Ruthie's."

Ruthie's was a cosy, informal restaurant off St Martin's Lane where musical theatre folk frequently gathered.

Ruthie knew how to keep the hoi polloi out so that the stars could eat in peace and chat about business.

"Not for long," Bella said reluctantly, knowing she ought to do as Charlie said.

Maureen said she knew about Ruthie's. She said that never in her wildest dreams had she expected to go.

Bella and Charlie closed up the Classic and they set off.

En route, Maureen listed her many performances in amateur dramatics, the regional accents she could do and the photographs a friend had taken so that she had something to send ahead for auditions.

"Ruthie's!" Maureen breathed in awe when they reached its unprepossessing frontage.

Bella almost expected the child to stroke the brickwork, and wondered if it was a wise thing to be putting Maureen among the famous; perhaps they should not be raising her hopes.

Bella pushed open the door and was immediately surprised.

She saw Lawson Garratt to her left, producer of a dozen hits, making a joke with a young man from "Salad Days".

On tables further inside sat a string of well-known actors and singers.

Charlie had been in the game long enough to know most of them and began to make his way through the maze of tables, Maureen's hand firmly in his.

"Toni!" he cried as he reached Antonia Quinlan, lead in some show about angels whose title Bella had forgotten.

"This is Maureen Godbolt, an actress from Berkshire."

Toni gave the girl a polite nod and Charlie moved on.

There was Johnnie Usk, even more handsome in real life than when Bella had seen him in "Annie Get Your Gun" in the spring.

"Maureen Godbolt, an actress down from the country," Charlie said, and Bella saw Johnnie look up and give Maureen one of his sparkling smiles.

The girl was stiff with excitement.

The restaurant was packed with famous faces, but then Bella remembered that it was snowing and the theatres were shut.

Even decent London flats in 1959 were not warm, so they had come to partake of the benefits of Ruthie's.

The room was long and narrow. Charlie snaked his way along with Maureen and Bella behind him.

Some people only smiled, but Bella was surprised to see that some leaned forward, asked Maureen a question or chatted briefly.

Ingrid Patrice (who'd made £50,000 in Hollywood last year in film musicals) examined Maureen's necklace, pronouncing it charming.

The diners seemed to be giving Maureen more attention than they were giving Bella herself.

They would often look up, see Charlie, see the girl, and something in their expressive faces would change by just a fraction.

"Nice to meet you," Harold Wills said in his booming voice, and kissed Maureen's hand.

Maureen kept glancing back at Bella as they made their way to a table near the back of the restaurant.

Charlie carried on.

"This is Maureen, a young performer visiting us at the Classic."

"Gerry! Can I introduce you to Miss Godbolt, a young actress staying in London?"

Then Bella saw her – Olivia Freidman, the biggest thing that year and recently engaged to a Danish nobleman.

Olivia shone like a polished diamond. She sat with a tall blond man whom Bella assumed was the Danish nobleman, and both of them were calmly surveying the restaurant.

Bella was keen to talk to Olivia; they had met briefly at a party and the Classic was now desperate to tempt her in.

Bella edged past Charlie and Maureen.

"Miss Freidman, I don't know if you recall my face from Nora Sanderson's in St Audley Street, but –"

"Of course I do," Olivia replied.

Bella sensed the other two standing behind her, looking like spare parts.

She turned to them.

"You'll recall Charlie Davis, my assistant."

But Olivia was looking at the hopeful face of the girl whose eyes were alight as she understood that she was meeting musical theatre royalty.

Bella remembered an article about Friedman in "The Stage", how she'd worked hard on chorus lines before her break.

"This is Maureen Godbolt," Bella said.

Olivia's gaze didn't falter.

"Oh, I know," she said in her husky voice.

Bella understood at last.

These performers, so many of whom had nursed the same dreams, had seen in Maureen's young face a reflection of themselves.

They had seen their old longing. It was just as Charlie said – people deserved a dream.

As for Miss Godbolt, she walked to Paddington Station that night on a cloud of air, with a new tone of confidence in her voice.

* * * *

Bella learned from her sister later that Maureen had got her break: a small part in a touring production of "Call Me Madam".

"She was a changed girl when she got back from London," Frances said. "We're all convinced the visit got her the break."

Then a note arrived for Bella at the stage door of the Classic.

It shared news and expressed gratitude.

When you're next at Ruthie's, it read, *give my best to the gang.* ■

Kintail, Highlands

The dramatic landscape of Kintail is breathtaking. From mountains and glens to waterfalls and lochs, its wildness attracts everything from otter to deer and magnificent golden eagles above. Little wonder, then, that nature lovers and hillwalkers are drawn to the area, with the skyline dominated by the Five Sisters, which offer magnificent views for those hardy enough to scale them.

One of the ridges, the Sgùrr nan Spainteach, or Peak of the Spaniards, takes its name from the 1719 Battle of Glen Shiel, when Spanish marines and Scottish Jacobites had to flee the advancing government forces. Eilean Donan Castle, just over half a mile from the old fishing village of Dornie, held a stash of gunpowder, so was blown up and left in ruins. The castle has been built and rebuilt over four times and a wealth of history is held within its walls.

Not far from here are the spectacular Falls of Glomach, which can only be reached on foot. Although it's a bit of a hike, with a drop of more than 370 feet, the falls are worth the climb.

No Crib
For A Bed

by Laura Tapper

ORNING, Reverend. Cold front moving in from the east.
Finally starting to feel a bit more like winter."

"Indeed it is, Mr Chapman," Eleanor replied with a smile, as
she opened the churchyard gate.

There were so many things about village life that ran as
regularly as clockwork, and Maurice Chapman was one of them.

Seven o'clock every morning, he walked down to the General Stores
for his paper, come rain, hail or blow, and he always had the latest
update on the weather.

When she had arrived from the city to take over the running of the
parish church, Eleanor had relied on people like Maurice to help her
settle in.

She'd found the congregation of St Margaret's, although relatively
small compared to her last church, to be faithful, welcoming and
committed. Eighteen months on, she already considered many of them
to be valued friends as well as members of her flock.

Cold from the iron ring handle managed to get all the way through
Eleanor's woollen mitten as she let herself in the heavy oak door. In
spite of all the warnings she'd been given by the church council, one of
the first changes she'd insisted on when she took up her post was
leaving the church door unlocked at all times.

"Theft is on the rise, vicar. It's always on the news these days – we
have a responsibility to protect church property," Mrs Watkins, the
treasurer, had cautioned when Eleanor had broached the idea.

"More important is our duty to provide a place of safety and solace at
all times of the day and night, for anyone who needs it."

A few members had needed some convincing, but she'd held her
ground and the ancient iron keys had hung on a hook in the vestry ever
since.

Her rubber soles made the slightest squeak across the red and black
tiles as she made her way to the altar. Following her morning prayers,
she turned and looked around the familiar building.

There were two weeks until Christmas and the ladies in the flower
committee had agreed to meet that morning to deck out the church in
its festive finery.

Illustration by Gerard Fay.

As her eyes roamed across the 18th-century box pews which had miraculously avoided Victorian renovation, something caught Eleanor's attention and drew her in for further investigation.

*   *   *   *

"We'll need to move the foodbank basket out of the way for the tree." Mrs Watkins walked towards the back of the church. "I suppose it would be good to hand the donations in, anyway. I should think they need all they can get at this time of year, poor souls."

"Actually, I think we should leave them here for the moment, Ruth." Eleanor hurried down to take the basket, but the treasurer had already picked it up.

"There seem to be some things missing, Reverend. I put some Jaffa Cakes in here myself. Did the toddler group borrow them? I've spoken to them about that before." She immediately began to bristle.

"I think we've had a night-time visitor." Eleanor gestured towards one of the box pews.

Mrs Watkins put the basket down quickly.

"Vermin, you mean! How awful! We'll have to ditch the lot."

"Not animal visitors, Ruth. A rough sleeper. The beanbags in the children's pew had been rearranged when I came in this morning, and the floor in the toilet was wet, as though someone had had a wash. It looks like someone came in here out of the cold last night."

"I warned you about locking the church, Reverend. I'm not one to say, I told you so, but theft is theft and I think this is a matter for the police now. After all, that food was donated in good faith . . ."

Eleanor put her hand on her friend's arm and spoke softly.

"This person must be in need of our kindness and support, Ruth. If we can't spare some soap, a few biscuits and a little space in our hearts, then what does this building stand for?" She picked up the basket.

"You're quite right about the tree, though. We can put this under the table where we put the nativity, so that people can carry on donating."

"Fair enough, Reverend." Ruth held her hands up. "It's your decision."

The band of women spent a busy morning decorating.

The tree bore a mix of decorations new and old, many made by the children, each window-sill was draped with evergreens, and the crib scene, which had been used for more years than any of them cared to remember, was set up on a slightly rickety table.

Eleanor picked up one of the battered Wise Men and cradled him.

"You really do look like you've been on a long journey. I wonder how many children have carried you around the church over the years?"

"Hundreds, I should think." Ruth smiled as she came and looked at the rest of the stable scene. "I remember the wonder on my children's faces when they held candles as we blessed the crib and sang 'Away In A Manger'. They've all got children of their own now."

Eleanor placed the character gently back on the straw. That sense of continuity had been a revelation to her since she'd left the hustle and bustle of city life and come to this village.

She knew that some of her views and ideas were challenging, but she never wanted her parishioners to lose those precious traditions which ran like a golden thread through the fabric of all their lives.

*   *   *   *

"Colder by the day, Reverend. Still might not get a white Christmas, though."

"Let's hope not, Mr Chapman!" Eleanor gave him a cheery wave.

Unlike so many, she never prayed for snow at this time of year. It looked beautiful on Christmas cards, but she knew how many problems it could cause: chaos for people trying to get to see family, injury for those who had falls on the ice, isolation for those who struggled to get out, and misery for anyone without a place to call home.

Not everyone was lucky enough to have chestnuts roasting on an open fire.

Eleanor always started the day with prayers, but that morning she couldn't resist peeking into the children's pew on her way past, just to see if there was any evidence of another visit in the night.

Sure enough, the beanbags had been rearranged again. The blanket and pillow she'd put in there the previous day had been folded back up neatly, but she could see that they'd been used and the flask which she'd left filled with hot tea was empty and washed out.

She'd also put some extras in the foodbank basket to boost supplies and, while she was assessing what had been used, she heard the door creak open behind her.

"Ruth!" Eleanor welcomed her friend. "You're out and about early."

"I thought about what you said yesterday, and I had a look through my cupboards." She held up a shopping bag.

Eleanor opened the bag to find a wide range of food items, toiletries and other things. It was clear that Ruth had been on a shopping trip specifically.

"This is very thoughtful of you, Ruth."

"It was looking at the crib scene that did it, really. I thought, what if one of my children found themselves in that situation? I'd hope that someone would reach out and help them. Like the innkeeper did with Mary and Joseph."

The two women put the food items in the basket and then stood side by side contemplating the nativity scene.

"It's wonderful to know that, after so many years of service and in spite of their worn-out appearance, these simple characters and their familiar story can still inspire us to live kinder lives," Eleanor mused.

"Hold on a moment, though." Ruth picked up a shepherd boy and examined him. "This little chap seems to have been spruced up for the season." She held him out for her friend to see.

Sure enough, the kneeling little boy had been repainted. His eyes were bright, his clothes were once again a sage green and his hair was brown all over his head, rather than being scuffed and scratched.

"It seems that we may have an artist in residence," Eleanor said. "Or else this really is a Christmas miracle."

*　*　*　*

From then on, Ruth met Eleanor every morning at eight o'clock and they continued to find evidence of St Margaret's nightly visitor.

Gradually, they thought of more things which would make the children's pew a more comfortable place to stay: a travel kettle, hot-water bottles, a radio, a collection of books.

As the days went by, the crib scene was transformed, one character at a time, to a beauty it hadn't enjoyed since Ruth had been a young woman herself.

The closer it got to Christmas Eve, the more heavily an important issue weighed on Eleanor's mind. Finally, on the morning of the twenty-second, she voiced her concerns to her friend.

"Ruth, I think we're going to have to cancel the Watch Night Service on Christmas Eve."

There was a long pause.

"Now, Eleanor, I hope you're not going to be offended by this. I realise that you've been dealing with this situation in your own way, and I've respected that − this is your church, when all's said and done."

Ruth swallowed, seeming to search for words.

"The fact is, I've been keeping the rest of the church council abreast of developments and we've already had a meeting. I think we all recognised that we might come up against this very situation."

Eleanor was stunned.

"You called a meeting without me? Is that even allowed?" She felt a lump developing in her throat. "I can't believe you would all do that."

Ruth reached out and placed a hand on her friend's arm.

"Now, don't distress yourself. Just hear me out." She drew Eleanor over to sit in one of the pews.

"None of us want to do anything to drive our nightly visitor into the cold, least of all on Christmas Eve, so we want to hold a silent candlelight walk through the village at midnight instead.

"We've all agreed to leave presents, here, for the person, whoever they are, after the crib service, and then we'd like to leave the church in peace until the ten-thirty service on Christmas morning." She winced a little.

"We realise it's not our decision, though. I hope you don't think we're interfering."

Eleanor felt the tears gather in her eyes and spill over on to her cheeks. Every time she thought she'd got to the bottom of these people, she found they had greater depths in their hearts, still to be discovered.

"That sounds like a perfect idea."

＊　＊　＊　＊

On Christmas Eve, the crib service was a joyous occasion.

As always, the children were invited to come along dressed up as any character they chose from the Nativity story and, if there were a few more Kings than were strictly required, nobody was counting.

Naturally, when it came to the blessing of the crib and the singing of "Away In A Manger", there wasn't a dry eye in the church.

Eleanor and Ruth shared a look at that moment, knowing how much more meaningful the tradition had become for them and how their unknown visitor had helped to enhance it for the generations to come.

In spreading the word about the candlelit vigil, an appeal had also gone out for gifts suitable for the church guest. A box wrapped in Christmas paper was placed at the top of the aisle and, during the singing of "O Come, All Ye Faithful", people brought forward their contributions.

There was a whole range of things, from selection boxes to socks, from a sketchbook to a scarf, all thoughtfully chosen and lovingly given. Eleanor placed two things in the box: a pay-as-you-go mobile phone, programmed with her number, and a short note.

To our dear artist friend,

Please accept these gifts with our love. Thank you for repainting our nativity set so beautifully – you have a real talent. You would be very welcome to come to the rectory for Christmas dinner, but I wonder whether there is somebody else in the world who is missing you.

Christmas is a time for family and forgiveness so, if there is anyone who loves you, please use the phone to ring them and tell them you're safe. Although I hope to meet you on in person on Christmas morning, I understand if you would rather not. Either way, have a safe and peaceful Christmas and contact me at any time, day or night.

God bless you.

Eleanor.

＊　＊　＊　＊

"Merry Christmas, Reverend. This bit of drizzle will clear by lunchtime."

"Merry Christmas, Mr Chapman!"

In spite of the much later start, Eleanor felt tired as she opened up St Margaret's to get ready for the Christmas morning service.

The turkey had gone in first thing and all the vegetables had been prepared yesterday, so she felt like she was on track, but it was always a lot to get organised when there were services to run as well.

This was where married rectors had the advantage, she thought. It was that extra pair of hands and someone to share it all with.

Still, she had four parishioners who would otherwise be dining alone coming round for Christmas dinner at half past one and she was certain they'd be fairly understanding if everything wasn't completely perfect.

She walked up the aisle to the altar and, out of habit, looked into the children's pew. The blankets were neatly folded, the flask washed out and the beanbags laid out to make a mattress.

"We did the right thing, then?"

At Ruth's voice, Eleanor turned round.

"It seems so. It was bitterly cold last night, so I'm glad they were in here."

The two women tidied everything away and, finding the gift box empty, assumed that the presents had been welcome.

Eleanor went through to the vestry to put on her surplice and stole ready for the service.

There on the table was a drawing, one sheet taken from a spiral-bound sketchbook. She picked it up and stared in wonder.

There was a curving line of people, all wrapped up in warm coats, hats and scarves, holding candles and looking joyfully serene, in front of a backdrop of trees and cottages on a beautiful starlit night.

Amongst the characters, she could pick out features that she recognised, and at the front of the line, without any doubt at all, it was her that was leading the group. She left it on the table to show Ruth afterwards.

Throughout the service, Eleanor reflected on how fortunate she was to be part of that community.

Bright faces shone up at her as they lifted the rafters with their singing and, when Maurice forgot himself and started singing an extra verse very loudly, everybody was more than happy to join in.

There were those who thought communities like this needed to move with the times, but the last two weeks had demonstrated how open-hearted and flexible they were.

All she wanted now was to have that extra guest at her table for dinner, because she couldn't bear to think of anyone sitting all alone out in the fields or woods on Christmas Day.

The table was set and her four visitors were telling each other their cracker jokes.

As Eleanor stood up to fetch the turkey, she felt her phone vibrate in her pocket. She had a text.

Rang Mum. Didn't think she'd want me back. There's a lot to sort out but we're going to try. Thanks for everything. Merry Xmas. Amy. ■

Lake Vyrnwy, Wales

This reservoir in Powys, built in the 1880s, stretches for four and a half miles and was created to supply fresh water to Liverpool.

The straining tower is the start of the 70-mile journey taking the water through three pipelines that run under the Mersey to Liverpool, and the structure wouldn't look out of place in a fairy-tale.

The huge dam took 1,000 labourers seven years to build, and the old village of Llanwddyn was sacrificed in the making of it.

King George V made an appearance at the official opening of the dam in 1910, staying at Lake Vyrnwy Hotel, which affords spectacular views from its high vantage point.

This Welsh valley offers fabulous walks, bike trails and water attractions, ensuring there are plenty of activities for those who flock here, keen to immerse themselves in the beautiful countryside.

You'll spot a huge array of birds from great spotted woodpeckers through to peregrine in the RSPB's nature reserve, which covers a huge 24,000 acres.